Short Grass

G·K
Hall
&Co.

Also by Tom W. Blackburn
in Large Print:

Companeros
El Segundo
Patron
Ranchero
Yanqui

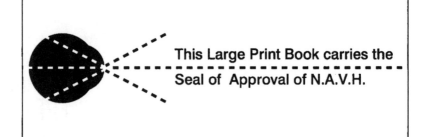

This Large Print Book carries the
Seal of Approval of N.A.V.H.

Short Grass

Tom W. Blackburn

G.K. Hall & Co. • Waterville, Maine

Published in 2002 by arrangement with Golden West Literary Agency.

G.K. Hall Large Print Paperback Series.

The text of this Large Print edition is unabridged.
Other aspects of the book may vary from the original edition.

Set in 16 pt. Plantin.

Printed in the United States on permanent paper.

Library of Congress Cataloging-in-Publication Data

Blackburn, Thomas Wakefield.
    Short grass / Tom W. Blackburn.
        p. cm.
    ISBN 0-7862-3963-8 (lg. print : sc : alk. paper)
    1. Large type books. I. Title.
PS3552.L3422 S47 2002
813'.54—dc21   2001051965

Short Grass

BOOK ONE

Chapter 1

Wind came in from the *llanos*. It came through the cracked gray poles of the sagging corral on the edge of the mesquite. It ruffled a dingy curtain in an open window along the little mud walled row of cribs below the corral and it whipped unclean wash on a line in the multiple dooryard before the cribs. Fine sand breathed unobtrusively against the worn clapboarding of the La Mesa Mercantile, and the slatted half doors of the Texas Pride saloon swung restlessly. Dust rolled against Les Macambridge as he came up the street, depositing grit in his ears, putting its taste in his mouth, and stinging his eyes. Macambridge swore at the dust and the wind, but the protest was automatic. There was always wind on the *llanos* and Macambridge had no quarrel with the sand in the air. The dust of North Texas was restless. It recorded a man's tracks, but it covered them, also. And it came out of an emptiness into which a man could vanish as simply and effectively as the wind itself.

Ducking under the clothesline in front of the row of cribs, Macambridge opened a closed door and stepped inside. The room was oppressive, sticky with heat and body smells and the accumulated offensiveness of time. Banta sat in a stiff rocker, the broken wicker seat of which had been carelessly repaired with a wadding of burlap. Banta was without shirt and shoes and his gun belt lay on the ragged quilt footing the chipped iron bedstead. The woman from whom Macambridge had rented the room was on Banta's lap. An empty pint of unlabeled whisky lay on its side on the stand at the head of the bed. Macambridge pushed the door closed with the flat of his back. He looked at the woman.

"I told you to keep away from us till we were through with this room," he said. "I told you this was business. Get out!"

The woman turned round jet eyes up to Banta's beard-stubbed jaw and wormed her fat, sagging body confidently closer to him. Macambridge reached the chair in one stride. He hooked a hand in the loose breast folds of the woman's untidy dress and yanked her to her feet. His left hand brushed across her face with smart impact, leaving the white tracery of the back of his hand across one round cheek.

"Get out!" he said again. "And keep your mouth shut."

Hand to her face, the woman scuttled to the door and slid out. Banta rose and dropped down on the side of his bed, above his boots. He pulled one of these on and looked up.

"A man gets lonesome, Les," he murmured.

"You take so damned long, getting a two-bit play set up."

It was an explanation of the woman's presence, not an apology. Macambridge carefully accepted it as such. La Mesa was virtually empty and certainly without interest in what occurred at the cribs. A woman's talk would not be listened to. No damage had been done. And Banta would not have opportunity to repeat his insubordination.

"Get dressed, Jack," Macambridge said. "We're set. Charlie Bissel's place is empty except for a drifter — a saddle bum. And the town is empty. Get down to Bissel's while that drifter's still there."

"I thought we were waiting till Bissel didn't have any trade at all," Banta protested. Macambridge shook his head.

"It'll work better this way. Bissel's been banking this part of the country out of his saloon so long he's spooky as a one-eyed mare. And he's rough, in his way. You go in and brace him alone and he's apt to see tracks. When I come in, he may be half expecting me. So we've got to shoot our way clear, maybe. And Bissel's got enough friends around La Mesa to make up an ornery posse if something happened to him. Pete Lynch and some others. We're dodging trouble. At least till we've got our roots down here."

"Hal said we was to jump Bissel when he was alone. That was all figured before we headed for town — all three of us voting the same way."

9

Uneasiness sharpened Banta's voice. Macambridge answered him with persuasive softness.

"Hal's back in the piñons, Jack, waiting for us to show up with the cash out of Bissel's safe. Enough cash to buy those five sections up for sale in Long Draw. It's you and me that are here. And I'm telling you how we do this."

Banta pulled on his other boot and started twisting into his shirt.

"All right, Les. How does it go, then?"

"Soon as this is over, you're moving south to pick up stock. You'll probably be on the move for the next year or two. It won't make any difference if Bissel sees you. You won't be here later to be identified. I'll be here, working the home spread with Hal and Randee, so I've got to keep out of the sun. You've heard about Bissel. He makes a point of keeping his place orderly. Won't stand for a tangle in front of his bar. The drifter that's in there now is good bait. He looks down to the frayed end of his pigging string. Belly as flat as a tin plate and likely as empty. Down on his uppers, but wearing iron and trying to keep his chin high. He'll be as ringy as a lamed bull."

Banta nodded amusedly.

"I walk in and put the prod to this bum. When Bissel comes out from behind his bar to break up the noise, you —"

"When Bissel comes out, you get him, Jack," Macambridge cut in. "A mouthful of knuckles or the barrel of your gun. Something to stiffen him long enough for me to get in and our business done and get out again without him knowing I was there. But don't plow him under permanently. We might need him again. The minute he goes down, I'll be in at the door."

"I'd feel better if this drifter wasn't wearing a gun," Banta said. "I might be busy with Bissel. You got to take the drifter off my back, Les —"

"I'll be watching from the door with my iron cocked," Macambridge agreed.

Banta slapped his belt across his hips and snapped the buckle. Lifting his hat from the bed, he dropped it onto his head.

"You'd be a bad man if you had guts enough to swing the dirty end of a stick yourself, Les," he said wryly. "This is the last time I draw the shag end in a piece of partnership business. I'm telling Hal the same thing when we get back to the ridges."

Macambridge nodded pleasantly. "All right, Jack. The last time," he agreed.

Banta stepped out into the sunlight. Macambridge eased back into the rocker and rolled himself a smoke with the deliberate relish of a man who has made a good trade. He was plumbing a pocket of his vest for a match when the woman whose cubicle Banta and he had used to keep off the street pushed open the door with a sister from the next stall behind her. The woman's face was puffy about the place where he had struck her and anger had lifted her temporarily above ingrained fear.

"Chirrionero!" she spat. "You stay and the other one goes. So you cheat me of a wage, too, eh? From now on I watch you. I find your business. Maybe I find your woman. Then I make you trouble. You like that, no?"

Macambridge's cigarette was alight. He flipped the match, still aflame, accurately across the room. It landed in the corner where the bed was jammed against the wall. A seam in the ticking of the mattress was open there, exposing the dusty straw of the filler. The match fired this. Flame leaped up. Shrieking, the two women leaped onto the bed and began pummeling at the fire. Macambridge crossed to the door.

"Like I told you," he said harshly, "you'll keep your mouths shut!"

Stepping outside, Macambridge turned unhurriedly up the brief street. Jack Banta was swinging rapidly along ahead of him, near Bissel's saloon. Midway down was the Mercantile, shuttered in the absence of its owner, who had gone out with his wagon to the county seat for a load of supplies. Except for Banta and himself, discounting the women in the shacks behind him, Macambridge knew the town was empty. His satisfaction grew.

Something never came from nothing without hard work, certain risks, and careful thinking. This was a good partnership — Hal Fenton, Banta, and himself. Fenton was a plugger, determined and bullheaded, but with enough sharpness to see the big stakes when they came up on the table. He knew cattle. He knew where he was going. And he had no qualms over methods. There was Hal's younger brother, dreaming himself into casting a bigger shadow than he really owned, but still old enough to make an extra hand when there was need. And Banta — Banta had been valuable in the beginning. He had an uncanny ability to locate cattle which could be moved quietly, quickly, and at a profit. And he was hard enough to bluff down pressure against them if it built too high. But now they had enough stuff in the ridges to work from. Their increase could be legal from here on if they could get the additional graze to feed it. And Banta had become a stray thumb — a little too touchy and a little too sure. If there would be trouble in the partnership, it would stem from Banta. Macambridge smiled. If — Hal Fenton was not the only man who could lay a plan.

Banta turned from the walk into the Texas Pride saloon. Macambridge lengthened his stride a little, watching his timing closely. Reaching the doorway of the saloon, he halted and silently parted the doors slightly, so that he had a view of the interior. Banta had been direct, even in this. No buildup at all. Riding through on a high, hard hand, the same way he worked with a horse or a woman. He had jumped the stranger at the foot of the bar as though picking up an old quarrel, renewed by a chance meeting. Macambridge watched the drifter's face register surprise, then fine down into a hard mask of swift anger.

"You're making a mistake, Mister!" the stranger snapped at Banta. It was more a warning than a protest. Banta bore down recklessly.

"You made yours when you lit down again in the same town with me. You're asking for this —"

Banta moved forward with arrogant truculence. Macambridge swung his attention to Charlie Bissel. The saloonman had ducked momentarily behind his bar. He came up with a length of maul handle in his hand.

"Hold it, boys!" Bissel protested sharply. "Outside with that — !"

"Keep out of this!" Banta growled, over his shoulder. "This bucko's got a pistol whipping coming and he's going to get it — right now!"

In the doorway, Macambridge drew and cocked his gun. The next instant was a flurry of motion within the saloon. Banta swayed his body and lifted his gun effortlessly in an apparently open attempt to make a clubbing pass at the man in front of him. The drifter, eyes alert, stepped sharply back. His hands dropped, but an element of surprise still obviously tempered his anger at Banta's bullying. Charlie Bissel, swearing heatedly, came over the bar in a clumsy leap, his maul handle high.

Banta was smooth. Changing footing and direction, he swung in close to Charlie Bissel and brought the barrel of his gun up in a sharp arc. As Bissel's feet struck the floor, the front sight of the weapon rapped solidly against the under side of his jaw. Bissel sagged and spilled off to one side. Weapon in hand, Banta wheeled defensively back toward the stranger. And as Banta swung, Les Macambridge fired carefully in the doorway. The bullet struck Banta in the back of the head and dumped him into the litter at the foot of the bar.

Macambridge pushed through the door, holstering his gun as he moved. The stranger jerked his attention from the two men on the floor, his eyes screened defensively. Macambridge grinned in an easy simulation of relief.

"Got him just in time," he said.

"For who?" the stranger asked bluntly.

"For you!" Macambridge grunted. "He'd have nailed you, sure — with your hands empty."

"You wasted your powder," the stranger said quietly. "He'd never have touched me!"

The statement was without vanity. Macambridge felt a curious uneasiness. He shook it off with an effort.

"Well, he's down and you're up. Add it any way you want. We'd better hit leather."

"Why?"

Macambridge felt a rising irritation.

"Ever hear of the law?" he snapped. The stranger smiled.

15

"Somewhere, I guess. But not on the short grass. Law doesn't grow on the *llanos*. A man makes his own as he goes along."

"Then stay here and make yours. When that bartender comes around, he'll remember you were tangling with the other one there, and I won't be around to swear you didn't put a slug into his head — from behind."

The drifter's crooked smile widened.

"Horse sense," he conceded. "I didn't figure this rut in the mud was exactly paradise, but I aimed to eat before I moved on. If you can lead me to a chuck wagon closer than a day's ride, I'll drift with you. I'd as soon have company as not."

"Bring the horses up in back, then," Macambridge said. "Mine's back of the corral — a bay with a shoulder blaze. I'll cover up here till you're back."

The stranger pushed through the curtained doorway leading to Bissel's living quarters in the rear of the saloon. Macambridge waited until he heard the outer door close, then doubled the end of the bar and squatted down before Bissel's open safe. It contained some papers, a tin change box, and three greasy cigar boxes. He found what he wanted in one of these. A thick sheaf of bills of various denominations — an accommodation kept on hand by Bissel for customers who were a long three-day ride from the nearest bank. Emptying the box, he shoved the bills into his shirt. Coming out from behind the bar, he knelt by Bissel and satisfied himself that the saloonman was still unconscious.

16

Macambridge was waiting at the back door when the drifter brought up the horses. The stranger's mount was a misbred, patchy, shag-coated paint with the loose-jointed walk of an animal which has been ridden too far too many days on end. So the man was a long drifter. A looking kind which seldom found the right bunk or the right graze. This was a final touch of per-fection. Macambridge figured he'd get this man well started across the *llanos*. In the direction of the Red River would be best. He'd likely keep going. Back in La Mesa, Charlie Bissel would hang the robbery on the stranger and in a while it would be forgotten. Out on the ridges, there would be just the two Fentons and Macam-bridge, quietly buying up the Long Draw sec-tions with Bissel's money. A tight partnership, building a big ranch out of nothing more than guts, powder, and the sparse, rich grass of the *llanos*. Hal Fenton, Macambridge knew, would be well satisfied with all aspects of the business he had done in La Mesa.

Macambridge whistled his way out of town. Just over the crest of the first swell beyond the empty street, his companion twisted in his saddle.

"Sort of cheerful for a gent who's just made somebody a nasty job of grave-digging," he remarked. Macambridge chuckled.

"My name's Macambridge. What's yours?"

"Lewellyn," the stranger answered. "Steve Lewellyn. If you're so damned happy, why don't

17

you sing? It couldn't be any worse than your whistling."

Macambridge felt a bite in this man. He felt something else, too. The uneasiness which had shaken him when he first stepped into Bissel's saloon. This man was no kid. A long kind, loosely built and hard. The kind to which youth clung. Reckless, certainly. Likely quick enough to temper and as quick in judgment. There was something in the eyes, in the set of the face — maybe even in the economy of motion with which Lewellyn rode which marked him. The mark of a man who could be dangerous. Macambridge instinctively knew this Lewellyn had a feeling for the right of things — principle, perhaps — and he had a limit beyond which he would not go.

Macambridge stopped his whistling. They rode on in silence, an irritating smile pulling at Lewellyn's lips. It lasted four or five miles, with Macambridge slowly bending their course so they swung closer to Pete Lynch's place in the bottoms along Willow Creek and farther from the brush camp on the ridges where Hal and Randee Fenton waited Macambridge's return. They had about reached the place where Macambridge figured he could cut off and let Lewellyn cut his own track alone when Lewellyn spoke without turning his head.

"Talkative as hell, aren't you?"

Macambridge was startled. "First I've got to find you a chuck wagon. Now I've got to amuse you, too."

18

"I doubt if I'd be amused," Lewellyn answered. "It just seemed likely that what's in you would come busting out and you'd get around to telling me what your count against the lad you nailed back in town might have been."

"The one that jumped you? Never saw him before."

Lewellyn shrugged slightly.

"You can't whistle and you lie worse. I saw you in the doorway when he first started to climb me. You were waiting for something. I never like to be pushed around for a blue chip in somebody's game unless I know what else is on the table. We'll let it go at that."

Macambridge scowled. Here was trouble. Lewellyn could talk when he met company again. Talk traveled fast on the short grass. It could come back, years later, with plenty of hurt left in it. Macambridge saw what the rest of it would have to be. He didn't think it would be too hard. Somebody'd find this Lewellyn out here on the slopes, face down in the sod. Finding him would only further cloud up the facts of what had happened today in La Mesa. In the long run, this was likely the best solution. First Banta — now, Lewellyn —

Macambridge was very careful. He continued to ride loosely, giving his companion no more attention than he had before, and he waited. The time was a long while in coming. It came on the bank of a cutbank with a notch only wide enough for one horse to slide for the bottom at a time.

He eased his mount unobtrusively a little to one side, as though the animal had refused the slide of its own volition. Lewellyn appeared to suspect nothing. He put his horse into the notch. In the moment that his horse was tilted sharply downward and the man's thighs were gripping his saddle so tightly that he could not easily shift, Macambridge drew and fired.

He was so close to his target that he could see the dust fly from Lewellyn's shirt. And when the dust was gone, he could see the small round hole the bullet left behind it. A small round hole near the center of Lewellyn's shoulder blade. The impact of the bullet drove the man forward and down across the horn of his saddle and his hat rolled into the dust. Macambridge eased with relief and started to let his gun down. In that instant, the incredible happened in front of him.

Lewellyn caught himself before he was out of his saddle. He rolled his shoulders. His gun came up from under him, its barrel lying back along under an upraised arm. Macambridge could see the dark steel of its muzzle. There was fire, sound. The recovery and the twist and the shot all seemed to come together. Macambridge knew it could not have happened, yet it had.

There was much else he knew in this motionless instant, but it did not have time to form completely in his mind. The flame of Lewellyn's gun engulfed him. It lifted him from his saddle. It was at once brief agony and an infinity of oblivion, into which he fell, headlong.

Chapter 2

In late summer, when the cattle had come in off higher ground to the bottoms in search of graze, Willow Creek ran dark with the muck cut up by their hooves and it took half an hour for a bucket of the water to settle out clear enough for drinking. There were leeches in the creek then, finger-long and voracious, and a week didn't pass without a thick-bodied diamondback showing up in the brush along the creek near the house. But this early in the year Willow Creek was clear and fresh and the deep pool below the ford was a constant invitation when the sun was high.

Sharon Lynch climbed out on the grass on the far bank and arched back in a shallow dive into the water. There was exhilaration in the mild chill and the rush of the water past her body. There was a freshness and a feeling of cleanliness which defeated the eternal dusty gray-green of the ridges reaching out to the horizon. Back at the near bank, Sharon rose from the water and came up the gravelly shingle to the edge of the grass. A large, use-softened towel and her dress and a can of soft soap were piled there. She paused and looked southeastward toward Long Draw. Her father and the two Mexican riders he employed had ridden out toward the draw after breakfast. They were not yet back in sight, which meant she would have at least an hour before they returned.

Picking up the can of soap, Sharon went back to the water's edge and began to lather herself. She used the soap prodigally — as a ritual and a luxury, rather than through any need. There was, she supposed, something wrong in these afternoon baths when the ranch yard was deserted, but she treasured them. The sun on her body daily browning it to an unmarred warmer tan, was a reminder of her youth. The water and the rich lathering of soap and the short, splashing dives into the creek were a delightful rebellion against the set pattern of a woman's life on this monotony of grass which offered a man challenges to match his labors but which held nothing for a woman beyond the changeless routine of her chores.

Lathered from head to toe, hair and body, Sharon tossed the soap up onto the grass and stepped back into the water. As she did so, she looked up. A horse was part of the way out into the ford above her, motionless. And the horse bore a man. A man with a slumped body and a pallid face turned toward her with unmistakable interest. Paralysis seized her. She had not kept an eye on the country to the westward. It was empty. She had not expected anyone to approach from that direction. There was no place among the ridges to the west from which anyone could come. So she stood for a moment, all soap and astonishment, unable to move.

The man reached awkwardly for his hat and removed it. His eyes smiled and his lips smiled.

"Excuse me, Miss —" he said so softly that his words were nearly drowned in the rush of the creek.

The smile did it. An admiring smile; honest and inoffensive, but a smile, nevertheless. Anger came up in Sharon and her paralysis fled. She took a forward step and launched herself in a flat dive. It did not quite come off. It was too flat; the water was too shallow. She struck the surface noisily, flinging up a soapy spray, and she wriggled frantically for deeper water like a stranded fish. Soap from her hair ran into her eyes and smarted. She scraped one knee on the sand of the bottom. But she reached the center of the pool and cleared her eyes and floated her hair about her on the surface like a screen.

Her dive had startled the horse in the ford. The animal was shying nervously. Sharon had surfaced with a lashing for this intruder on the tip of her tongue but she withheld it in fresh astonishment, watching the man. His hat had escaped him and was floating on the current toward her. He had lost his reins. They trailed into the water from the bit. And he was gripping the horn of his saddle with both hands in a peculiar sort of desperation. The shying of his horse rocked him in the saddle. He glanced once toward Sharon with a look somehow apologetic, then his head canted limply forward, tension ran from his body, and he tilted slowly forward and down into the water.

The current across the shallows of the ford rolled his body once before Sharon saw the shocking stain of blood which covered almost the whole back of his shirt. She struck out then, swimming against the current, and was into knee-deep water when the creek brought the man's body to her. She caught him under his arms, bending her back to his limp weight, and dragged him ashore. She left him on the gravel, his boots still in the water, while she ran to the edge of the grass, dropped her dress over her head, and hurried back with the towel. Rolling him over, she pulled up his shirt and wadded the towel over the hole in his shoulder. The blue rimmed wound had begun to bleed again, darkly. She knew she could not drag him farther. The strength of neither would be equal to that.

Leaving him again, she ran toward the house. There was a dilapidated barrow in the wagon shed. Stumbling, running, she wheeled this back to the creek. The barrow tilted unreasonably and the man's body was heavy, the more difficult to handle for its limpness. And the barrow's narrow wheel cut deeply into the sod when she tried to push it up the small rise toward the house. When she reached the dooryard she was sobbing for breath and a wild fear was in her. Fear that the man would die — that he would die now, while she was alone with him, before her father and Diego and Manuel returned to the house.

Sharon was afraid of death. Miserably afraid. There was blood on her arms and she was sick.

The man's boot heels raked up the little braided rugs on the floor of the front room as she dragged him across it and his wet clothes left a trail of water on the planking. She had trouble getting him past the stove beside the kitchen door and when she had rolled him onto her bed in the little ell off the kitchen she thought she could do no more. But there was a blue tinge creeping into the pallor of the drawn face and she realized he was chilling.

It was not a thing a woman did, but she stripped the wet clothes from him and heaped every quilt and blanket on the place high on the bed. The chill seemed to subside. She wasn't sure. But she could think of nothing else. Going onto the porch, she searched the horizon in the direction of Long Draw. Far off across the gray ridges, she saw movement. She felt heartened. Her father was on the way back. Pete Lynch was an old man and a tired one, but he was wise. The *llanos* had made him so. He would know what to do.

Sharon went back into the kitchen and sank down in a chair at the table. She looked at the face. It did not belong to a boy, but it was young. Stretched thin with pain, she could learn nothing more from it. Rising, she hung the wet clothes behind the stove. She lifted the belted gun last. She did not like its weight. She did not like the cold beauty and symmetry of the weapon, but she pulled it from its holster and carefully dried the barrel and grips with a kitchen cloth. Going to her father's battered desk, she returned with a ramrod and a cleaning patch. She ran this through the barrel and methodically ejected the cartridges in the cylinder, drying each chamber as she emptied it. The fifth contained an exploded shell. The sixth chamber was empty, after the universal habit of saddle men. Sharon looked a long time at the fired shell, then dropped it into the firebox of the stove and shoved the live cartridges into empty loops in the nearly full cartridge belt from which the holster hung. Placing the gun on a shelf, she went back to the chair at the table.

Presently her steadiness returned and she found her mind going back to the scene at the creek, searching details for something to ease the returning sting of her embarrassment. She remembered the man's smile and his eyes. Particularly his eyes — stricken, glazed with hurt, but seeming to say: "Beautiful — beautiful!" as they looked at her. Cleanly, the way they might look at a tall tree or antelope on spring graze or a thunder tower against a sunset when the late summer rains came. And the hat — he had taken off his hat.

It was hard to sit in a chair with the quick, light sound of a wounded man's breathing in her ears and the torment of questions the coming of a stranger on the *llanos* always raised, and be able

26

to do nothing about it beyond waiting. But Sharon had schooled herself. Her judgment was most severe against herself. She hoped she had iron; she needed it. But of another kind. A conviction that justice was not an individual judgment nor the execution of it an individual prerogative. A conviction that the frontier of which she was a part had but a single road by which it could reach the orderliness necessary for full settlement. A road milestoned by sober meetings and problems quietly discussed, not by the bodies of men dead of personal quarrels and the hot, proud flaring of heady angers.

These were her beliefs. She had nursed them since she could remember, hating her helplessness, schooling herself to patience and a tight control over the sickness of body and spirit the flaring of violence left in her. Her father would not need her forever. There would come a time when she was free of her obligation to him. And because she was a woman and would be young, even then, with beauty and her self as weapons, she would have power — at least over one man. If she chose that man rightly when the time came, she could do much through him. This thought sustained her when waiting was bitter — as it was, now.

The man under the blankets on her bed continued to breathe with sharp and painful shallowness. Sharon continued to wait until she heard her father and his two men ride into the yard. She went to the door. Manuel was leading the wounded man's horse. They had already been down to the ford, then. Her father swung down from his dusty horse and came up toward the house with long strides, his saddle gun in his hands with its hammer eared back.

"It's all right, Pete," Sharon called from the porch. "A stranger. Fell out of his saddle at the ford. I've got him in bed in the kitchen. He's asleep. Maybe he can talk when he's rested."

Pete turned to his waiting riders.

"Turn the horse in with the others —" He came on up the steps, his eyes on Sharon. "How long ago did he show up?"

"About an hour. With a bullet in his back. He'd come a long way with it."

Pete pushed past her into the house and ducked through the low kitchen doorway. He did not turn toward the bed. His eyes traveled from the wet clothes and the brass laden belt hanging behind the stove to the shelf on which Sharon had put the wounded man's gun. Lifting the weapon, he spun the empty cylinder. His eyes jumped to Sharon.

"Unloaded," he grunted. "You handle this?"

"I dried it," Sharon said carefully.

"No brand on the horse; no smoke in the gun. But a bullet in the back. I don't like it. I hope he can talk."

"I said he was sleeping, Pete."

Her father made no answer. He stripped the blankets back from the man's bare torso. With a gentleness which too often betrayed him, he felt

28

about the chest area where the bullet had come out and rolled the man's body slightly to examine the hole over the shoulder blade. There was skill in the examination, but it was short. Pete Lynch replaced the blankets and pulled off his hat.

"He ain't sleeping, Honey," he said wearily. "He's unconscious — out. It's been a rough day, eh?"

"He's going to die?"

Pete nodded and turned back to the man on the bed.

"You could tell by where the holes are, but let that go. How the hell he ever sat saddle after he took that is beyond me. Go by the breathing and the color. Either one's enough by itself. Poor devil! He's finished."

Sharon was staring at the man's bloodless face. The eyes opened suddenly. They reached up at Pete with a shadow of mockery. A vestige of a grin pulled at his lips. There was an instant in which the marshaling of strength was an obvious effort in him. Then his lips moved and a question came faintly.

"Want to put a blue chip down on that?"

Pete snorted astonishment and bent forward. The man's lips continued to move.

"Go away. I don't want a nurse — with whiskers —"

The eyes swung to Sharon. The smile grew wider for a moment, then faded. The wounded man closed his eyes again.

Pete shrugged out of his vest and peeled back the cuffs of his shirt.

"You've got water on. Good! Get me your scissors and something white that's clean that I can cut up. Then get out front and stay there unless I holler for you —"

Chapter 3

Lewellyn waited until the hoof roll of Pete Lynch's horse had faded before he swung his legs over the side of his bed. He had been lying for nearly two weeks in changes of Pete's drawers. Pete was a shorter man and rounder in the middle, so the drawers made a funny fit, too short in the crotch and inadequate as hell, everyplace else. He looked at his arched, boot-shaped feet and the blue veined thinness of his legs. This was a poor exchange for his first glimpse of Sharon — one flash of heaven in an afternoon of hell already mercifully receding in his memory — but he had to have his clothes. And two weeks with Sharon around him had convinced him there was only one way he would ever get his gear.

He started gingerly across the floor. He was a little unsteady, but not quite as wobbly as he had feared he would be. The thing which troubled him most was the sagging stiffness in his shoulder. Not a hurt exactly — hardly even a discomfort most of the time. More a tight singing of nerves imbedded in knitting flesh, alive with a constant warning that there was a short limit to what these muscles could do, now.

Lewellyn paused in the kitchen doorway to

assure steadiness, then stepped on into the front room. Sharon had just come back in from the front porch. She stared at him incredulously, then with half anger.

"What are you doing up — like that?"

Lewellyn looked downward at himself and grinned at her.

"You get back into bed!" Sharon said firmly. Lewellyn continued to grin and moved toward the front door.

"I want a look at the sun —"

Sharon watched him take a pair of strides before she smiled.

"For heaven's sake, all right! Sit down and stay away from that door till I find your clothes. Diego and Manuel are down the yard somewhere. They're not as used to you as I am. I don't think they could stand you like that!"

The chair was welcome enough. Lewellyn sank into it.

"Not very grateful," he accused. "I figured I owed you something like this to even the score."

Sharon was at the clothes press in the corner, her back to him. She didn't turn, but he saw the color rise on the back of her neck.

"I told you I'd poison you, Steve Lewellyn, if you ever mention that — that afternoon again!"

She turned, dumped his carefully pressed and folded clothing onto his lap, and went into the kitchen, pulling the door sharply closed behind her. For all of her color, there had been laughter in her eyes. Lewellyn chuckled. A man rode a

32

long trail, sometimes, to find the quiet eddies where enjoyment came easily.

Dressed, feeling strangely uncomfortable in his own clothes, he was still chuckling when Sharon came back in from the kitchen. She surveyed him critically.

"I think a horse could bear looking at you, now," she decided. "But don't get any idea you're ready for a saddle, yet."

Lewellyn shook his head and thrust his hand into the slack in the waistband of his pants.

"No," he agreed ruefully. "Got to take care of this, first. What's to eat?"

"An hour after breakfast?" Sharon protested. "Isn't there anything to a man but dirty clothes and a kitchen table?"

"Not much, I guess," Steve conceded. "Born in trouble, live in trouble, die in trouble — it adds up to about that for most of us, I think. And it's a woman who's hurt. It should be different."

"Can it be?"

Sharon's eyes were suddenly somber, serious, almost pleading. Lewellyn, who had been relishing the lightness they had between them, felt a stir of regret. But he answered her honestly.

"I don't know."

Sharon sat down facing him. She pulled one of Pete's shirts from the table onto her lap and threaded a button. She did not look up.

"Pete said you'd die, Steve," she said. "Even I know that you should have. But you didn't. Why?"

"You'd done enough. I didn't want you digging my grave, too."

Sharon brushed this aside.

"Was it because you'd left something undone? Something you wanted to do. Was it because you'd been shot — in the back?"

Steve made no answer.

"You've never told us how it happened — who it was —"

"No," Steve said. Sharon put down her sewing.

"All right, Steve," she said. "I'll not pry into that, then. It doesn't concern me, I suppose. But this does, and I want the real answer. Why did you get up today? Why not yesterday — or tomorrow? Was it because today Pete is riding into La Mesa for the first time since you came here?"

Steve tilted back in his chair. A man could not sidestep inevitability.

"I passed through La Mesa the day I fell into your creek, Sharon. Pete Lynch would never ask a sick man to move on. I guess I wanted to save him that. I wanted to be on my feet when he came back."

"That's all you want to say, Steve?"

"That's all."

Sharon was silent for a long moment, her long lashes down over her eyes and her high, cool forehead furrowed with thought.

"Do you know why Pete went into La Mesa today?"

Lewellyn shook his head.

"There are some relinquished homesteads bounding us over in Long Draw which can be bought up for the county taxes. We've wanted them, but a snakeskin outfit up in the ridges has wanted them, too. So Pete stepped out of the way."

"Because you wanted him to?"

"Because I wanted him to. Yes. But the ridge outfit hasn't made any move. Even I can keep Pete waiting only so long. He has a friend in town who has a little money. He's gone in to see if he can borrow enough to buy those sections in Long Draw."

"What about the ridge outfit, then?"

"It's a partnership. Three men. Hal Fenton, Leslie Macambridge, and John Banta. They're new in here. We've never even seen Banta. We don't know them. We can only guess."

"Sometimes guessing isn't hard."

"Yes, I know," Sharon said. "But Pete is a man. He can sell himself anything he wants to believe. I'm worried, Steve."

"There's something I can do?"

"If you will. No one in La Mesa could have put a bullet in your back. Your trouble wasn't there. I'm sure of that. I want you to stay. Regardless of the story Pete brings home or what he says to you, I want you to stay here. I want you to help him."

Lewellyn shrugged.

"A man who doesn't want help can't be

forced, Sharon. But if Pete will have me when he gets back, he's got another hand for as long as he needs one, spurs, saddle, and gun."

Sharon's face deepened.

"He doesn't need a saddle hand, Steve. And the gun — you don't understand. Pete says a cattleman is born wise to stock and the grass. And he says you're a cattleman. He respects your opinions. Try to keep him from building something too big out here. He's getting old. This isn't what I want when he's gone. He doesn't belong out of shallow water. Keep him clear of trouble. Don't let him tangle with that outfit in the ridges over the land in Long Draw."

"I'll talk to him — if he'll listen," Lewellyn agreed. "If the ridge outfit has got first rights in Long Draw, I'll try to keep Pete out of it, for you. I couldn't do it any other way."

Lewellyn knew Sharon was not satisfied with this, but he had his own convictions and his own knowledge. On the *llanos* there was only one road into trouble and one out. A man had no choice. Pete Lynch would go as the wind blew, as his luck led him. A man always did.

Sharon rose and headed toward the kitchen.

"You said you were hungry —" she murmured.

Pete Lynch rode home with the sunset, sitting a little twisted in his saddle as a tired man will. Lewellyn watched him come in across the home bench and dismount at the corral. Manuel came out of the bunk shack to look after Pete's horse. Pete spoke briefly with Manuel, then turned up toward the house with a slow stride. Sharon ran down the steps and met him in the yard. Pete kissed her affectionately and they came on together. None of it was misleading. Lewellyn waited patiently in his chair.

As they came onto the veranda, Pete threw Lewellyn a quick, challenging look and touched Sharon's arm.

"Get supper on," he said. "I want to talk to Steve."

Sharon glanced at her father and sank onto the veranda rail.

"I think I want to hear this —" she said quietly. Pete shrugged and turned to Lewellyn.

"Charlie Bissel's safe in his saloon was cleaned out the day you rode in here, Steve," he said carefully. "Charlie and me spent the day putting our cards together. Here's how they came out. Banta, one of the partners in the outfit on the ridges above Long Draw, came in while you were in Charlie's place and jumped you. He played it like he'd known you before. But Charlie's a hard one to fool. He figures now you'd never seen the man before, that Banta was using you for bait. Anyway, it looked like trouble. Charlie came over his bar to quiet it and got Banta's gun in his face.

"When he came to, you were gone and his cash was gone and Banta was dead on the floor. You showed up here a few hours later, back shot and buckling at the knees. So somebody must have got both you and Banta from behind while Charlie was out, and you dragged yourself this far after they'd beat it with the money. It was something like that, Steve?"

Lewellyn looked at Sharon. She was watching him with a peculiar fixity, caught in a struggle between curiosity and an aversion for the details of violence. Perhaps there was distrust in her, as there was in Pete. Distrust and caution. A stubbornness would not let Lewellyn ease it. His ride with Macambridge was done. The fare had been paid, both ways. And that ride did not concern Pete Lynch or his daughter.

"Something like that," he nodded to Pete.

Lynch stepped into the doorway of the house with something like relief on his face, as though he had expected no more than half an answer and so was satisfied with what he had heard. Sharon rose after a moment and followed him without comment. Steve heard her presently in the kitchen, dishing up supper from the stove. Pete almost immediately reappeared on the veranda and squatted down on his heels beside Lewellyn's chair.

"This isn't for Sharon," the old rancher said swiftly. "Get her out of this yard and what she knows or understands about the *llanos* wouldn't cause you trouble in your eye. I wasn't the only one in La Mesa today, Steve. Hal Fenton was down from the ridges. Banta was one of his partners. Somebody found the other one — Les

38

Macambridge — out on the grass with a center hole through his shirt pocket. Hal won't miss either one of 'em. He could buy 'em both coffins and be plenty ahead, what with the ridge outfit all his, now. He just figured there was somebody on the flats fast enough to be watched. Banta and Les Macambridge had been lads who could handle themselves. Maybe Hal was spooked a little on account of that. I kept my mouth shut, but I reckon I could have told him where to look —"

"Why didn't you?"

"Because I wanted the answer to one question from you first. Did you take Bissel's cash out of his safe?"

Lewellyn shook his head. Pete's eyes brightened.

"We'll haul up right there, then, son. That's far enough for me. If there's anything else, it's your business. I was set on making a loan from Bissel. He's clean, so that's out, now. But I still aim to hook onto those sections in Long Draw. I want 'em as much as Fenton does and I've got to clinch them before he does. You got to grow in this country. And my string is playing out. I'm thinking of Sharon. I got to pile up something here for her. So with a loan from Charlie out, I've got to turn someplace else. Maybe take in a partner, or something. I've got a notion you'd fatten up on this grass, Steve."

Lewellyn understood perfectly. A man made strange compromises on the *llanos*. Pete Lynch knew Fenton's partners had made a try for

39

Bissel's money. He knew they had failed. And he was reasonably certain Lewellyn could lay his hands on the money. His one question had been sop to his conscience. If Lewellyn had not actually robbed Bissel's safe, to hell with the rest of it. That money would still buy land.

"You'll find some bills rammed into a pocket in the lining of the skirt of my saddle, Pete," Lewellyn said quietly. "I don't know about this grass, but if there's enough cash there to do you any good, you've made yourself a deal."

Pete rose, nodding satisfaction. He offered his hand.

"We'll get along, Steve."

Lewellyn glanced down the length of the veranda, momentarily ignoring the outstretched hand. He smiled slightly.

"We should, as long as you keep on coppering your bets, Pete," he said wryly. "Think you can call the boys off and send them down to wash up for supper, now?"

Pete colored darkly and slowly turned. He glanced back at Lewellyn, then grinned. He raised his voice a little.

"It's all right, boys. Tomorrow you start taking orders from Steve the same as from me —"

There was movement at the end of the veranda. Manuel Cosa and Diego Aguilar rose from hiding there. Both looked a little uncomfortable. They holstered drawn guns and moved down the yard together with obvious relief.

Lewellyn leaned forward in his chair and took Pete's hand. When he looked up, Sharon was standing in the doorway of the house, watching them both. There was no way to tell how long she had been there.

Chapter 4

There were thirty-two hundred dollars in the lining of Lewellyn's saddle skirt. A crumpled sheaf of bills which Pete Lynch brought undisturbed into the kitchen long after Sharon was asleep in the outer room in order to count them in front of Lewellyn. Enough to clear the Long Draw sections and to add some needed equipment and a head or two of breeding stock to Pete's own investment in the ranch. Pete was outspoken in his enthusiasm. Lewellyn was mildly astonished to discover that under the impetus of this windfall of cash Pete was younger and more spirited than he had earlier thought.

With the possibility that Hal Fenton would discover a way to move into Long Draw, Pete was impatient. He was up early, saddled and with his trail-gear packed. He promised Sharon and Lewellyn a quick trip and an early return. Steve was not overjoyed. He had not tired as much as he had expected on his first day up, and the prospect of the better part of a week with Sharon and himself alone in the house was pleasant.

However, Pete was still in sight, far across the benches, and Lewellyn was still beside her on the veranda when Sharon made a difference in this.

"Before Diego and Manuel start down the creek this morning," she said quietly, "call them up here, Steve. I want them to carry your bedding down to the shack. They can rig up another pole bunk for you and you'll be comfortable, I think."

"You want to be alone in the house?" Steve was surprised.

"No. I hate being alone in this country. I always have. But I think you'd better move."

"Pete wasn't worried. Why should you be — or maybe it's so the neighbors won't talk?"

"Do you think what neighbors might say would make any difference with me — if we had any?"

Lewellyn looked at her — the widely set eyes, the pride in her carriage, the large, strong mouth — the full, firm, proud figure she made against the brilliant sunlight beyond the eaves of the veranda. He shook his head.

"No. You'd make few friends among neighbors, I guess. I don't think you'd care if you made enemies. You'd only care that you were right. That's it, isn't it?"

"Call Diego or Manuel. I want to get my own bed moved back where it belongs."

Lewellyn laughed softly.

"It couldn't be that now I'm on my feet, you're afraid of me — ?"

Sharon turned clear eyes on him. Her head tipped a little back.

"There's one thing you should know, Steve

43

Lewellyn; one thing you should remember. I'm not afraid of any man alive. I never will be!"

Steve reached out for her, then. He pulled her to him and bent toward her still upturned face. Her lips were momentarily hard and angry under his. He had meant this all casually, but a sudden harsh aggressiveness seized him and Sharon wilted before it. She clung to him with almost a wildness and in this moment Lewellyn, with a man's slowness of perception in some things, understood her loneliness and bitterness and the constant, impotent hatred she nursed against the kind of life to which she was bound on the *llanos*. He released her and stepped back. . . .

"Always be a little afraid of everything, Sharon," he said gently. "Even kittens have teeth, and you never know when they'll sink them in you." Turning to the steps, he went down them, calling across the yard:

"Diego — Manuel, *venga aquí!*"

Lewellyn spent the day at the bunk shack, rebuilding the rope-sprung bunk the Mexican hands had rigged for him and straightening up the disorder of the room enough to make it bearable. The noon hour came and passed with no attention from Sharon. The hands returned in late afternoon and washed up noisily in the trough under the bottom bar of the corral. Presently they came on to the shack and paused together, just within the door, surveying the unaccustomed orderliness.

They glanced at each other. Diego, heavier

44

and older and more sure of himself than his companion, scowled at Lewellyn. He swept the interior of the shack with his hand.

"We got to keep the sleeping place like this?" he complained.

"Working a saddle is not enough? We got to scrub and sweep, too? Maybe Manuel and me, we don't like a job with two bosses!"

"Specially when you've got to sleep with one, eh?" Lewellyn chuckled. "Climb off the high horse, Diego. You boys liked the shack the way it was. I like it this way. It's up to me to see it stays cleaned up, then. Fair enough?"

Both men looked relieved. Manuel eyed Steve closely and finally spoke, choosing his words with care, but with humor surfacing in his eyes.

"So you don't care for the sleeping at the boss house, eh, *Señor* Lewellyn?"

The inference was plain. Lewellyn, a border man, knew his border people. Gallantry was understandable, but seldom seen. It was, therefore, fertile ground for the making of jokes. He grinned.

"You're both *Tejanos*. All three of us wear the same size boots. Let's say I liked sleeping in the boss house too well."

The two riders laughed.

"*Seguro*," Diego agreed knowingly. "It is enough to make a man sweat. A peach on a cholla stem, for a fact. This is no country for a woman who can fit her backside into a small saddle. So much wanting in the eyes. *Ai*, there

45

are days when it is difficult to ride for Señor Lynch, even for me, who have had too many women!"

"Too many?" Lewellyn murmured. "You don't look dead yet to me."

It took no more than that. It was as lonely in a bunk shack as in a boss house on the short grass. Men had their vanities and the strange satisfaction of idle talk. To understand this and to share in it forged an easy bond. And beneath it lay the secure knowledge that Pete Lynch's two men would ride a hard trail into hell for Sharon without demand beyond recognition of their service. The indefinable aura which made a lady of a woman and the lack of which branded a harlot was nowhere so readily recognized or so generally respected as on the dun grass of the Texas plains.

When Sharon rang the triangle outside the kitchen door, Lewellyn moved toward the house between Diego and Manuel, and each of them, with exaggerated attempts to avoid the obvious, held down the pace to Steve's necessarily lagging strides.

Sharon was brisk in the kitchen, serving up the meal in silence. She relayed last minute orders left by her father to Diego and Manuel, but she ignored Steve. Nevertheless, he was content. He felt her eyes often upon him.

The meal finished, Lewellyn idled in the kitchen after his two companions returned to the yard. Sharon worked around him, making him feel the inconvenience of his presence. He ignored this, smoking a cigarette out in silence. When he was finished, he snapped the dead smoke into the woodbox and swung toward her.

"What's the matter?" he asked quietly. "Yesterday you asked me to stay on here. Today you moved me out of the house like I was poison."

Sharon sat down on the edge of the table and looked at Steve for a moment. Rising again, she crossed the kitchen and returned with his gun, which had remained on a kitchen shelf. She put it down on the table in front of him.

"I don't know anything about you but what I could see in your face, the day you came in here. And that wasn't much. Just the same, when I dried your gun, I emptied it, and I never told Pete what I found in it. You know what that was."

Lewellyn shook his head.

"No —"

"A fired shell, Steve," Sharon said. "I don't know too much about how men handle these things, but I'm not altogether a fool, either. I've lived too long on the *llanos* for that. I'll tell you why I moved you out of the house. You killed Jack Banta in La Mesa the day you came here. You killed Jack Banta and you robbed Charlie Bissel's safe. You lied to Pete, Steve."

"A killer, a thief, and a liar," Lewellyn said slowly. "That's a steep count. If I were you, tallying that kind of a score, I'd have moved me farther than the bunk shack, Sharon."

47

"I think I should," Sharon answered.

Lewellyn lifted the gun and balanced it in his hands. "Then why didn't you? Why don't you run me clean off the place?"

Sharon's eyes dropped. She bit at her lips.

"I — I don't know —" she said with difficulty.

Rising, Lewellyn shoved the gun under his belt and grinned.

"Whether you like it or not, girl," he said, "I'm afraid we're two of a kind. It's you who are lying, now —"

Turning, he pulled open the door and stepped out into the night.

Chapter 5

The third morning after Pete Lynch left for the county seat, Lewellyn had Diego Aguilar saddle a horse for him before the two riders left the ranch yard. A little after ten, when heat rose in the shack and the temptation of wind in his face was an added urge, Lewellyn pulled himself up onto the waiting animal. The effort taxed him and he knew he was riding a little too soon, but inactivity was a burden he had never borne gracefully.

It amused him to see that Sharon was not ignoring him as completely as she tried to make it appear. As he reined away from the corral, she ran onto the veranda of the house, one hand partially raised as though in protest. Lewellyn tipped his hat to her in a faintly mocking gesture. The upraised hand fell. He rode past within a rod of her. She said nothing. She did not return his salute. But when he was half across the bench reaching out from the yard, he glanced back. She was still motionless at the rail, staring after him.

Lewellyn's ride was essentially a survey of Pete Lynch's holdings, which he had not yet had an opportunity to view as a whole. But it was also an opportunity to think with the familiar motion of a saddle under him. The picture was plain enough. So were his own problems. He had hit La Mesa with nothing. Behind him were other towns, other benches across which he had already ridden. Behind him were old quarrels, long since settled, but their scars remained, troubling like old wounds when his thoughts moved across them. The country about La Mesa was so familiar that he would not have needed the curious events of his welcome into the country to realize that here, also, was the short grass — that here were other quarrels.

Not that quarreling was in the air. Lewellyn was always too close to reality to accept the ephemeral as explanation for anything. He knew where the roots of trouble grew. Friction thrived in the rich soil of a frontier expanding too rapidly for the operation and laws of a government designed for the close boundaries of an older farm-and-trade country. The physical space of the *llanos* made their own problems. Until free graze was gone on the short grass, there would be men building private empires out of sweat and sod and six gun. There would be men who hired and men who hired out. Some would be big and some small. And only a few would last.

Lewellyn knew his own course — if he stayed in the grass country. And he knew the risks. A man had to be hard as the next — a little harder. He had to be as quick. And in the last analysis, he had to be always right. He supposed justice was the right word. A man had to measure himself against justice and keep always in its shadow. This did not mean always the shadow of the law. It meant mostly that a man could keep his own respect only if he stood by principle. And principle here, as anywhere, was cleanly cut; a man bought what he sowed.

So it was move on. It was drift back toward the big rivers and the small farms. But toward timber and the rail lines and little green valleys busting their galluses with a big-eyed idea of their own little tin-plated importance. Back to hills that closed in on a man and small towns where there was a need for small talk and self-defense against little jealousies and the nagging disagreements which came from sitting helplessly — with a neighbor at either elbow who had full knowledge of your business and an assumed right to meddle in it.

Or there was to stay on the grass.

Even before he had hit La Mesa, Lewellyn had not had much doubt as to the limit of his drifting. Each man belonged to a kind of country. And when he thought occasionally about it, he realized that he had long had a private purpose astir in him. Order would eventually come to the *llanos*. He wanted his part in establishing that order, but according to his own lights.

Now his reasons for staying in Texas had multiplied. Pete Lynch had taken him in when he was seriously hurt. A debt existed because of this. And there was Sharon. It was for Sharon then — and for Pete, because he was Sharon's father — that he was staying. For Sharon and for

Pete and for himself. What he built here, if he could build at all, would be Pete's in the beginning. It would be Sharon's, later. And on the last roll of the dice, if the spots came his way, all that Pete left would belong to him.

By midday Lewellyn had a good enough picture of the land Pete owned along Willow Creek. Not the best land on the *llanos*, but good enough for men who would work hard. A fair beginning. A ranch with a chance for survival, even against the rough competition of fluctuating markets, bad years, and the grueling drive necessary to get beef up to the railroad reaching slowly out across Kansas, to the north. Satisfied with what he had seen of this lower ground, Lewellyn turned away from the creek and angled toward the ridges. He had no difficulty identifying Long Draw. The name fitted only the wide, grassed barranca which cut deeply into the main ridge with a sharp, precipitous weather wall on the north and east to afford natural shelter from the run of storms. There was water in the draw, chiefly underground. Lewellyn saw half a dozen green oases against the lighter dun color of unwatered grass which indicated springs or seeps at which watering tanks could be dug. And the specific sections Pete wanted were plainly outlined by the forlorn tracery of poor fences, gone to hell, and a few rank weed patches where a plow had turned a little sod under.

Lewellyn swung toward the home place in

midafternoon, speculating on the peculiar stubbornness of men who would homestead such country in the beginning. There was growing land and grassland and desert on the *llanos*. The last was useless and would remain unused. But there was profit on the rest of it if it was used right. A sharp stockman did not graze cattle on bottoms suited to hay. A sound farmer did not turn under in the hope of a more profitable crop. And it took a fool to file on a single section of either kind of land in the hope of making a living from it. But still the sodbusters came, drifting widely here and there. They raised their fences and broke their ground. They sweated in the sun and starved in the winter. And in the end they moved on again, older and with nothing to show for what they had spent on the *llanos*.

Half way down the length of the draw on the way home, Lewellyn saw two men wind out of the bush and rein up on the trail to wait for him. He studied them as he approached. One was small, very slight of build, young and almost womanish. The other, although not a big man, had the full, settled weight of maturity. An unlike pair, but with similarity, nevertheless. Lewellyn drew up before them, aware that they had been long waiting — that this was no chance meeting — that he had been watched and possibly even hunted.

"Howdy —" he said carefully.

"My name is Hal Fenton," the older man said quietly. "This is my brother, Randee. We're from the ridge. You're from Pete's place?"

"Steve Lewellyn." Steve made the acknowledgment terse.

"Where's Pete?" the older Fenton asked bluntly.

"I wouldn't know," Lewellyn answered.

Fenton nodded. "No, you wouldn't," he agreed. "A man riding the town trail keeps moving, and putting your finger on him ain't easy. Randee and me know that, Lewellyn. We figured Pete might be pulling out for the county seat, once he'd got back to his place from La Mesa. But he must have slipped past us."

Fenton stopped and ran calculating eyes over Steve.

"Lamed, ain't you, Lewellyn?"

"Some."

"Les should have done a better job on you than he did."

Lewellyn understood the reference to Macambridge. An impersonal, callous condemnation of the dead man. He smiled a little. "He was hurried a little, I think. A little too anxious."

"Les was like that," Fenton conceded. "Fool enough to be afraid of Jack Banta and want him out of the way, but not sharp enough to see danger in a gent like you. Les and me were different, Lewellyn. I don't move that fast. I don't hurry. And if I'm anxious, it don't show. Slow, maybe, but I get where I'm going. Les had Bissel's money in his shirt. You must have been hit hard. You missed three bills caught in a fold

54

under his belt. They were still there when we found him. I wanted that money. Les had it. Then you had it. Now Pete Lynch has got it. It ain't going to do Pete any good. I want this grass in Long Draw. I aim to get it. Understand?"

Lewellyn nodded.

"You've had your look at it, today," Fenton went on steadily. "It's good grass. You've seen that. What I want to know is if you think there's enough of it to let two outfits build up from its roots."

Steve turned slowly in his saddle and looked back up the draw. He shook his head. Fenton smiled a little.

"Then when you going to clear out?"

"When the creek dries up, I reckon."

Fenton nodded. "I figured you'd stay. Pete's girl, maybe?"

"That makes some difference?"

"No. I want the grass. That's all. Women make trouble when you trade for them. Put your iron on the Lynch kid if you've a notion. A man's got his own tastes. But watch yourself. And tell Pete you've seen me. He'll understand. If he don't, tell him I'm offering him a year's note for what he paid to clear title to these sections at the county seat. I'll give him a note for enough to add up a little profit and the expenses of his trip. But he's got to get out of the draw."

"Pete could be stubborn," Lewellyn suggested.

"Plenty stubborn," Fenton agreed. "Specially

if he's got a hard-head to back him. I've figured that in. If there was room for both of us in here, I might make another offer. But there isn't and I like my trouble early. My iron is going to be the only brand back of La Mesa. If you have trouble convincing Pete, bring him out here when he gets back. I'll have a thousand head on this grass by then."

Fenton tightened his reins and pulled his pony about. Lewellyn watched the two brothers ride off, but his attention was not on the older man. It clung to the kid, Randee, who had not spoken. There was an element in silence at a time like this which was compelling. Hal Fenton was likely the brains of the ridge outfit, but Lewellyn eyed the low slung guns at Randee Fenton's hips and he knew the boy was the more dangerous of the pair in any sudden thing.

Filing this observation with the mass of like impressions which a man gathered in a day and which added across a period of time into the sum of his experience and the soundness of his judgment, Lewellyn set his mount into motion again and continued on toward the Lynch place.

After supper that night, Lewellyn broke the self-imposed silence he had observed since Sharon had revealed why she had moved him out of the boss house. Shoving back in his chair, he turned to Manuel and Diego.

"You boys ready to start working for me?"

Manuel showed concern. "Work, *Señor?*" he

56

asked in astonishment. "Is it not a little soon for work?"

"I can sit saddle," Lewellyn said.

"You can wait for Pete, too!" Sharon cut in, drawn in spite of herself.

"I could. But this job won't wait. Come on, boys. We'll put our chins together at the shack. This chore'll need an early start —"

Crossing to the shelf on which Sharon had long kept his gun, Lewellyn reached down his brass-laden cartridge belt. With this looped over his arm, he led the way out of the kitchen. Sharon sat with clouded eyes at the table, but she said nothing.

Lewellyn had been troubled on the ride back from Long Draw by some uncertainty over Diego Aguilar and Manuel Cosa. Loyalty was one thing, practicality another. The concern was needless. Diego and Manuel readily recognized the situation and his plan for remedy. Relieved, Lewellyn left the bunk shack after half an hour for the quiet of a smoke in the night air. Lights were still up in the kitchen of the boss house and he saw Sharon's silhouette caught in the glow straying onto the veranda. She did not rise as he came up the steps. He settled himself in an empty rocker.

"Want to talk?"

"I think so —"

"Your deal, then —"

"Why are you staying here, Steve?"

"Because you asked me to."

"I mean — really?"

"I'm looking for another safe to open and somebody else who needs a bullet in the back of his head."

Sharon grunted soft disgust at Lewellyn's parrying. "I wanted an honest answer."

"From a liar? You don't need an answer. You know what it is. You're the reason. Supposing you let me ask the questions. You're not happy. Why?"

"Who is happy on the grass?" Sharon said bitterly. "Pete? The few friends I've known here? My dead mother, maybe? None of them, Steve. This isn't a happy country. It's wild and reckless and savage. People weren't made to live like they do on the *llanos*."

"No?" Steve said quietly. "I was. A wild country, all right. Maybe reckless. It's a kind of wonderful country, just the same, Sharon." He tilted his head toward the bench beyond the yard, lying shadowed and highlighted by a strong moon. "There's room, if nothing else. Room's important. If a man's going to grow, he needs it. A woman, too. Closed up in your clapboard kind of town, a man just thinks he throws a big shadow or a little one. He doesn't really know. He just goes by what he thinks — whether he's big or little. But when he's got to stack himself against flat miles and standing ridges and the wind running loose across half a county, he's got his own size out where he can see it. That's something.

"You've talked about peace to me. I reckon I want it down here as much as you do. But I know where it's going to come from. You don't. In a town you can take a man's gun off and put him in a Sunday suit on week days, but you haven't got anything but a lot of men corralled together. Men don't like crowding and you haven't taken their cussedness off with their guns. The trouble's still there — jealousy, greed, ambition, and just plain bad nature. Always will be. Out here, storms blow up. But when they're over, everybody knows where his peg is on the barn wall. When enough storms have howled themselves out, the nights'll turn quiet again, like they were in the beginning, and this'll be a place to be."

"The clean, free air —" Sharon mocked wryly.

"That's right," Lewellyn agreed. "The clean, free air. Freedom to heel a snake when you see one instead of being held by a book which says the critter's got to clamp a strike into your leg before you can start counting the rattles on its tail."

"Men aren't diamondbacks, Steve."

"Some are."

"You could make a mistake."

"Not with the ones I've seen —"

Sharon shrugged wearily.

"So that's what this is in the morning — a snake hunt?"

"Kind of," Steve said. "I met Hal Fenton and his kid brother this afternoon. They've got a little trick up their sleeve to surprise Pete when he gets back. I never mind using the other gent's deck. Where there's one trick there's two, and a surprise for a surprise is a fair trade."

Sharon rose from her chair.

"I know better than to try to stop you, Steve, but you've got to understand me, too. I'll never have anything to do with something that was bought with a gun."

Chapter 6

The sun was barely above the crest of the main ridge when Lewellyn pulled up in the Long Draw bottoms. He dismounted under a scarred cottonwood and pointed out the vague line of the old homestead fence which separated the uppermost of the three sections Pete Lynch wanted from unfiled grass above.

"Get a stump or a good gouging stick and rig a drag between your saddles," he told Diego and Manuel. "Haul it along that line so we get a clean, fresh mark that a man can't miss. When you're done with that, come back here. And don't take too long. We may be a little short on time."

The two riders went down along the line and found a scrub fence post which suited them. Presently they were riding abreast along the old fence line, their drag kicking up a cloud of dust behind them. Lewellyn walked down to the beginning of the line. It looked good enough. He went back to the cottonwood and waited. His two companions were back in twenty minutes. Lewellyn tilted his head at a rock outcropping some distance up the slope behind him.

"Stake out your horses behind that rock. Find some shade along it somewhere and watch all of that line you dragged. Keep your saddle guns with you. We're going to have a little company — this morning, I think. If a man or a single beef crosses that line anywhere, cut loose. *Sabe?*"

Diego nodded. "The ones from the ridges, eh? Then the next time we are in La Mesa on business of our own, we stay on the walks if we like? We keep the women we have chosen if it suits us?"

"You keep whatever you've a right to from here on," Steve said.

Manuel swore softly and with satisfaction. "Then we are not Mexicans, the way it is said to us in La Mesa?"

"Sure, you're Mexicans. But you're *Tejanos* — we're all Texans — in La Mesa or anyplace else. And we're going to make it stick. We don't hunt trouble and we don't run. Remember that. If one of you starts something, even if he has it handwhipped, all by himself, he's going to have trouble with me when it's all over. But if the start is somebody else, get word to me. I'll snake you out if it takes two lengths of rope. We work together."

"There could be danger —" Diego suggested.

Lewellyn laughed shortly. "You'll eat danger and you'll sleep with it," he said. "But before we're through, you'll be drawing pay from the biggest ranch in the country."

Manuel tilted his head up the valley.

"Somebody coming —" he murmured. Steve made a sharp gesture. The two hands put their horses against the slope back of him and rode in among the rocks. Lewellyn eased back in the cottonwood shade. Dust lay heavily in a notch where a smaller canyon cut into the upper reaches of Long Draw.

Time dragged slowly. There was not a large herd of cattle under the dust. Mostly scrub, coming down from poor grass above, by the way the animals kept scattering out on the graze of the upper draw. Fenton had boasted a little in claiming a thousand head ready for movement. But the count was unimportant. A single milker would be enough for this.

Directly, Lewellyn could identify Hal Fenton and the younger Randee. In addition, three other men were flanking the drive. They worked hard at their business and in half an hour the first of the animals had been pushed almost up to the line Diego and Manuel had dragged across the draw. Lewellyn leisurely mounted and rode down to it. He was sighted. The two Fentons separated themselves from the drive and pulled out ahead. The drive halted. Lewellyn met the Fentons at the dragged line.

"You get out early for a cripple, Lewellyn," Hal Fenton said.

Lewellyn smiled. "I'm not that crippled."

"You should have let this go," Fenton went on dispassionately. "It has to happen, sooner or later. With Pete gone, this was the best time — the next best thing to nailing Pete on his way. We might have done that, but he started too soon for

63

us. And now you block us. I told you I'd give Pete a note for these sections. Eventually I'd pay the note, too. The railroad is building fast across Kansas, now. When I've got enough fat beef on the hoof to make a drive worthwhile, I'll move it north and sell it off at one of the rail towns. I'll have cash, then. Pete wouldn't be cheated, in the long run."

"No. Except that he wants this grass. When beef is driven north out of this draw, it'll be wearing his brand. That's his answer."

"Which you're making for him?"

"That's right."

Fenton shrugged. He nodded at the line gouged in the earth in front of him.

"What's this, then?"

"Qualification under the law," Lewellyn said drily. "It's the owner's duty to fence his land. Until he does, he's open to trespass. I had the boys throw up this fence this morning. I figured you'd be along."

Fenton laughed.

"Pete wouldn't have thought of that," he said. "He'd know better than to haul in the law. What law is it, Lewellyn? Who's going to make it stick? A sheriff who hasn't got the guts to ride into this half of the county? A judge who can't read his own law books? You're the law in these ridges, and so am I. So it boils down to who's got the best brand. This isn't a fence; it's a scratch in the ground. This law you talk about says a fence is a barricade sufficient to prevent the drift of ani-

64

mals. One step and I'm across this. So are my cattle."

Lewellyn matched the man's laugh. "It's your beef and your neck," he said with a grin. "That line just looks like it isn't a fence. I'll lay you even odds that whatever crosses that line can't get back under its own power. It's that kind of a barricade. And I think it's good enough to hold you and your beef, both. There are a pair of rifles waiting up there in the rocks to see you test it."

Randee Fenton made the first sound Lewellyn had heard him utter, a sharp, explosive oath. At the same time, he moved. A smooth, lethal, long-practiced reach for his gun which betrayed the fact that young Fenton fancied himself one of a kind which had become legend on the *llanos*. Men whose natural skills and an incredible perseverance had been funneled into a single channel, whose guns were invincible. To Lewellyn, whose own youth and his drifting and his cautious friendliness had forced him into a similar pattern, the boy's hard competence and surety were startling. If physical speed and steadiness of nerves were virtues, Randee Fenton was a saint.

"This is a blue-chip bet, Lewellyn!" Randee snapped. "You had your warning. You should have seen enough yesterday to keep out of this. What's coming now is what you've asked for. How much good are your rifles up on the slope going to do you while I've got a gun in your belly? Start the stuff moving again, Hal.

65

Lewellyn'll stand still."

Steve met Randee's eyes levelly.

"The rifles on the ridge have orders to cut anything down that crosses this line. What happens to me is out of it. You haven't got a chance, Randee."

"Put that damned iron up, kid!" Hal Fenton grunted irritably. "There's a place for everything and we're not playing with Pete Lynch. Save your scares for when they'll take. You've got us on the short end, Lewellyn. They're your cards."

Steve nodded, but he continued to look at Randee Fenton. His eyes flickered to the boy's gun.

"Remember something, Randee," he said softly. "There never was a gun so fast there wasn't a faster one, somewhere. Don't ever punch iron into my belly again unless you're ready to ride it out, right then!"

Young Fenton stepped back a little, grudgingly, and holstered his weapon. His eyes remained on Lewellyn. His brother leaned down in his saddle.

"I'd sooner seen this settled now," he said. "It'll have to wait from here till I've made a drive and got something in my kick besides promises to hold my boys together. But there's still only room for my outfit here. I stick to that. When the time comes, I don't aim to trade quietly. All the chips are going onto the table. And I'll play hard. There'll be hurt and the play won't last long, Lewellyn. My offer of a note for Pete's title stands till then, but there'll be no warning when I withdraw it. Think that over."

Then Fentons had moved their cattle half a mile back up the draw before Diego and Manuel came down from the rocks. Manuel was openly admiring; Diego had a look of speculation on his face.

"That was a brave thing," he admitted grudgingly. "But maybe not wise. To now, these ones from the ridges, they are maybe a little rough in La Mesa — but we do not have to go into the town. And maybe they make big talk about how the boss will not be long on his grass — but we do not have to listen to talk. Now it is different. This is not talk, it is trouble."

"Is there any difference between talk and trouble but a little time?" Lewellyn asked. "Would the Fentons leave Pete Lynch alone forever?"

"No," Diego agreed. "I don't think it. But when a man does not have trouble, does he look ahead to see when it will come?"

"If he wants to hang on, he does," Lewellyn said flatly. "Tomorrow you two get back up here. Patch up what fences are left on this upper section so that we've got something across this line that'll hold stock. As soon as you've got that done, cull the herds on the benches below and run the best stuff in here. Stuff you think Pete would cull for a drive to the railroad. This grass is good. It'll put on weight that will stand a hard drive, even. Fenton says he can't move until he makes a drive and has a little cash. He means it. And we're in the same fix. We can look that far ahead, at least."

"*Seguro,* the fence can be mended. But why talk of selling cattle and of money? If the boss has money, it will be stolen from him."

"No," Steve said. "You don't figure the Fentons right. You don't see where Hal Fenton is headed. If he needed money in a hurry and Pete had some, Fenton would take it all right, if he could. But it would be a loan, even then. It would be repaid. Fenton is no thief. He's more dangerous than that. He's a man trying to build something. He aims to have a ranch in the ridges. A big one. What stands in the way of that will go down. Our one chance is to grow faster than he does — faster, bigger, and tougher."

"Me, I am not such a tough man," Diego protested.

"What would you have done if young Fenton had shot me and the rest of them had started across our line a while ago with that stock?"

Diego looked surprised.

"Do? Why, I had the little one in the sights of my rifle from the beginning. He would have died where he was. And if there were not more cattle than Manuel and me have shots, there would have been no live cattle on our side of the line."

Lewellyn laughed.

"You're tough enough, *compadre,*" he said.

"I'll take long odds that Pete Lynch runs a bigger iron in this county than the Fentons ever thought of before we're through —"

Chapter 7

Pete Lynch was gone six days. He came back with cleared titles to the five sections in Long Draw and a lading bill for a load of equipment which followed him a few days later by freight wagon. His enthusiasm was high. Lewellyn saw him looking often at Sharon with a pride in his eyes which was not because of her but because of the things he was doing for her. There was a wryness in this, for Steve knew that there was nothing Pete could build on the *llanos* which Sharon would want when her father was gone. Nevertheless, Steve felt the tide of Pete's eagerness and shared it a little. When there was a thing which could be built — when the tools and the material were at hand, a man wanted to get at it. In the end he did not figure what would happen to it when he was gone, and within limits, he didn't care.

Pete listened to Steve's quiet account of the brush with Hal and Randee Fenton. When it was finished, he eyed Steve levelly.

"That's the beginning," he said. "When the last hand comes, can we still hold cards, Steve?"

"It's a no-limit game," Lewellyn answered. "I don't see why not."

Sharon spoke abruptly from her side of the table.

"Do you have to make a gamble of everything — both of you?" she asked. "Even of building a ranch?"

"Life's a gamble, Honey," Pete said gently. "You think Steve or me could change that?"

"You could try," Sharon said firmly. "Somebody has got to. There's got to be a change. Somebody has got to make the first move toward it. Why not one of you — both of you? You think I could raise a family in this house, Pete? You think I could sit here, day in and day out, watching my men ride off and not knowing whether they'd come back sitting up in their saddles or dumped cross-ways over them? Not knowing whether somebody wouldn't come in at night on a grudge and burn the roof over my head? You think I could keep on cooking and sewing and watching forever and telling my kids this was the country God made for us?"

Pete grinned a little.

"Now, I don't know about that, girl. A woman's got a way of moving fast. Who's been talking about a family, about kids? Steve, I thought you stayed at the bunk shack whiles I was gone."

Sharon colored deeply, but she clung to her point.

"A little land and peace is better than all of the *llanos* and continual war," she insisted. "We've lived without the grass in Long Draw. We could

71

keep on living. When you put the sections up the draw behind our fence, we'll run more beef, Pete. But some of us may not keep on living. It's not right!"

Lewellyn stirred.

"Man wasn't made to walk backwards. Pete bought those sections. He doesn't want to sell. That's enough. If it isn't, look at it this way, Sharon. Fenton shoves him off up here and he goes, taking Fenton's note. He gets his money, eventually. Fenton will pay off. But he's backed Pete down, once. Directly he gets a notion he wants this stuff on Willow Creek, too. His part of the country is getting too small to hold him and he needs more room, more sections under his iron, more beef in his herds. Not for the money. For the feel of it — the bigness. So he comes down across the benches, making another offer and backing it up so it'll stick."

"Is Willow Creek the best graze in the world?" Sharon asked. "If a little profit could be made in selling out, why not? Why not move on? There are other places and with the money from a sale here, you could buy somewhere else, Pete."

"Because there are Fentons everyplace a man could go," Lewellyn said. "You can't get away from them. Gents with no lid to their ambitions. Weeds that won't stop growing. Sooner or later, wherever there's grass, wherever there's oil, wherever there's copper, the same thing comes up. You've got to dig in at the beginning. If you don't, you're done. Backing up is a thing that gets to be a habit. And nobody ever backs up a hill."

"The Fentons' kind are only half at fault," Sharon said grimly. "The rest of it is that there are Lewellyns and Pete Lynches everyplace on the grass, too. There are things in this world that are worth as much as being right in everything!"

Sharon rose and went blindly out onto the porch. Pete watched her go with a puzzled frown.

"When she was little," he said slowly, "she was a heller. I could see her and me getting along first-rate. But she's more like her mother, specially since you showed up here, Steve. And damned if I know which is her off-side, anymore. Seems I always rile her. What's the matter with her? What's she mean — things worth as much as being right?"

"She's a woman, Pete," Steve answered. "What does a woman want? A home, I reckon. Kids. Maybe neighbors — a preacher and a butcher and a post office. She just doesn't see that the rough time has to come ahead of the smooth."

"No, I reckon she don't," Pete agreed. "Look, son, Sharon'll keep for a spell. Likely she feels better for spouting some. Let her do it. We got a stack of chores ahead of us —"

Pete Lynch had sound ideas for the organization of his expanded graze. Steve understood the physical problems and how to whip them into shape. Both worked steadily. Steve found saddle work increasingly easier and he added daily to his share of it until he was riding the sun into the sky and out of it again. Pete had been accumulating the makings of something big on Willow Creek for a long time. The grass in the draw was the final addition. The trick now was to put the whole together into something which had life.

With Diego and Manuel grumblingly accepting added work, and with Pete and himself working harder than any hand, the Willow Creek ranch began to take shape. Benches were separated, catalogued in their minds, so they knew where they would move each bunch of beef as the cattle cut down the grass. The animals themselves were culled and culled again until each bunch was composed of like animals, grading from a scrub bunch to the tight little herd composed of the best market beef on the place.

Occasionally there was a meeting with a man from the outfit on the ridges. There was no friendliness with the Fentons or with the sullen men who rode for Fenton pay. Like a distant storm the feeling of friction and the inevitability of a clash were constantly in the air. But faced with their own labors, both outfits worked through a time of truce, each strengthening itself as fast as possible.

As Pete's ranch took on form and weight, Lewellyn felt his own body slowly building back to its own standard, daily repairing the damage Les Macambridge had done with a bullet in the back. And as he moved more freely, Lewellyn felt the weight of authority at Willow Creek shift imperceptibly from Pete Lynch's shoulders to his own. Pete seemed genuinely grateful for this, and as it continued, he brightened, his enthusiasm increasing daily and his confidence rising. Aguilar and Cosa, tightened now into an efficient pair who earned their pay twice over and who seemed to have acquired a personal interest in their labors which had been lacking in the beginning, made no attempt to disguise their preference in bosses.

Lewellyn met his change with a peculiar admixture of feelings. He was too practical not to realize that there was satisfaction in holding the reins of anything, whether it belonged to him or not. But he could see ahead. Successes would be his; so would mistakes. And the weight would grow heavier. He thought of Sharon. She had generally avoided him, keeping him always at a little distance since her father's return. And he knew that the growth of the Willow Creek place was, in her mind, a thing which had occurred because of him. He was therefore at once satisfied and disturbed. He had stayed on Willow Creek because of Sharon. And by staying, he knew he risked turning her fully against him. He was barefooted on broken glass and he knew it. But he could do nothing beyond waiting in the hope Sharon could understand him or he her. Either would be sufficient.

The season moved swiftly. More than three months after Lewellyn's arrival in La Mesa,

Diego Aguilar signaled Pete and him up out of a bottom in which they were working onto a rise. When they joined him, he pointed off to the east. A haze of dust lay across the *llanos.* A larger haze than Lewellyn had expected, and rising in an unmistakable pattern. Dust churned up by a Fenton herd strung out in the beginning of the long drive north to market in a Kansas rail town. Pete scowled.

"So he beats us off on the drive," he muttered.

"We had to wait for him," Lewellyn answered. "A checked bet is best in a tight game. Hal won't move against us till he can pay wages for the kind of work he wants done. He can't pay wages until he's sold his beef. So until he started this drive, we had time of our own. Now that's done. We'd better cut our own herd and shove it north, too."

"I'd have liked to wait two weeks, Steve —" Pete said.

"So would I. The stuff would weigh in heavier in Kansas if we could. But we've got to be sold out and ready when the Fenton crew gets back. Things will come fast, now."

"I'm going to handle the drive, Steve."

"Why? It's a rough trip, Pete. There's a long dry crossing. It's all day in the saddle and all night on the sod. It'll wear you."

"That's part of it," Pete said. "You've still got a hole knitting in you. But that's not it, really. One of us has got to stay here. I can peddle the beef. I'm a tolerable trader. But if hell busted loose while you were north with the herd, I

76

doubt if I could hold it down, here. I'd stake a round bet you could. That's why I want you to stay. And if that isn't enough, son, there's Sharon. Getting an honest answer out of her is like pulling teeth, now. But if I could, I've got no doubts as to how she'd answer. You're staying, Steve."

A day and a half behind the outfit on the ridges, and taking another trail, Pete Lynch and the two Mexican hands started Willow Creek's herd north to the rails. Steve watched them move down the benches without regret. He was glad enough to avoid the punishment of the drive while his wound was still stiff, and Pete was rugged enough to make the round trip without too much discomfort. Too, he thought Pete's judgment was sound. Both of them believed there was little likelihood of a move against them from the ridges until after both drives were done, but the chance always existed. And if there was trouble, Lewellyn wanted to be on Willow Creek when it came.

There was also Sharon. Pete was so sure that Steve would eventually marry his daughter that it made the whole thing difficult. There had been no chance to talk with her father. Now, with work eased and Pete absent —

Lewellyn had anticipations, therefore, but he was not prepared for Sharon's directness. The air had grown more thin with the advancing season. The first night after the departure of the drive, Steve found it cold in the bunk shack after supper. He was at the chopping block below the corral when Sharon joined him. There was still a trace of the sun in the western sky, lighting the one horizon while the other was sunk in dark shadow. Sharon stood silhouetted against this luminosity. Between strokes of his ax, Lewellyn watched her, sensing again the strange blend of blind, righteous strength and passionate, headstrong love of life which had drawn him to her in the beginning.

It was a comradely night, down tight on the *llanos*. Sharon was aware of Steve's attention. She stood, almost consciously posing, until he had finished splitting his wood and the light was almost gone. When he lifted an armful of fuel, she swung in beside him and they walked in silence back to the shack. She followed him through the door with little attention to the raw masculinity of the room. Aware that talk was coming and unwilling to hurry it, Steve built a fire. Sharon sank into Manuel Cosa's bunk, returning the stare Lewellyn had given her in the outer light. But she did not speak until Steve had dropped onto his own bunk and had built a cigarette.

"If I asked you to leave the *llanos*, Steve, would you go?" she asked suddenly.

"Alone — ?"

"No, with me —"

"Where?"

"A town, maybe. Someplace in Kansas. Not

too crowded. I wouldn't ask too much. One of the little homestead towns just getting their beginning. A place where we could start again, too."

"You're asking me to go?"

Sharon was silent for a moment. "No, not yet. I'm thinking out loud, Steve. Trying to see a way out of this for you — for me. You're going to fight the Fentons when these drives are over. Not for me. Not for Pete. Not even for yourself. You're going to fight them because they're trying to grow over the top of Pete. And if Pete was somebody else, you'd still fight them. I admire that, Steve. But not the way you aim to fight. That's where the wrong is. A man can't be judge, jury, and executioner. But you'll try — unless you go where the law has provided these things. Unless you go where there are other ways of fighting than with a gun."

"The same thing again, Sharon?" Lewellyn murmured. "Then the same answer. What a man fights with isn't as important as what he's fighting for."

"I don't want to argue," Sharon said. "You haven't answered my question, Steve."

"Sure," he said. "I'll go. I want to, Sharon. We'll leave Pete here. He can work out his troubles with Hal Fenton. He won't need us."

Sharon looked up with deep hurt in her eyes.

"You don't have to be blunt," she protested. "I've thought of Pete, too. That's why I said I was thinking out loud. We can't leave him. I see that. But I want to, Steve —"

She rose, crossed to the stove, and backed up to it. With an unconscious gesture, she lifted the back side of her skirt enough to let the red heat from the glowing stove strike the backs of her knees.

"No," she said after a moment. "Maybe it isn't what I want, after all." She looked at Steve. He rose from his bunk and moved toward her. She dropped her skirt and raised her hands slowly. She came into his arms when he reached her with a swiftness which was almost fierce, feeding strength of desire to his strength. Her arms were tight, her mouth soft, and her body against him not limp with surrender, but proudly aggressive.

"Steve —" she murmured. "— Steve, I want you. I love you, Steve. Let's not quarrel. It is so little I ask — and I want it so much. Help Pete make a deal with Hal Fenton — please help him —"

The warmth of the shack, laden with the smell of burning piñon, of old, oiled leather hanging from wall pegs, of sweat-salted working clothes and the brush on the hill, closed in around them. There was breathing and the clicking of the stove as heat varied with the draft, and the sound of the flames. There was restless movement of the horses in the corral and the soft rush of wind on the slopes and the wail of coyotes on a distant ridge. And over these things, there was silence.

Chapter 8

The front part of the boss house was quiet and the kitchen stove cold when Lewellyn went up for breakfast. Sharon was sleeping. Lewellyn made himself a cold meal and left quietly. When he had saddled at the corral, he ducked back into the bunk shack for his belt and gun.

Riding out across the home bench, Lewellyn angled into the sun toward Long Draw. The wind was fresh in his face and well-being was something which was alive in him; something which Sharon had built out of her sudden tenderness, her eagerness, and the honesty with which she had revealed the full tide of her love. Lewellyn felt a little incredulous in the morning light and unquestioningly sure of what he must do.

Old certainties stirred restlessly in him — judgments formed in a decade of drifting on the *llanos*. Each echoed warning. Warning that no man could make a truce with trouble. But Sharon's bid was stronger than convictions. There was no trouble, yet. And a man on the move was not always running.

Going up through Long Draw, Lewellyn found the upper line fence cut in two places and forty or fifty head of brush-scarred cattle on the grass inside. Scrub cattle, not worth inclusion in the Fenton drive and promptly run in onto Lynch grass as soon as Pete and his two hands had started Willow Creek's own market bunch north for the rails. Lewellyn had expected to find something like this. It bolstered Sharon's urgency, last night. Time to make peace grew short.

Lewellyn had not before been into the Fenton yard, but he had no difficulty following a scuffed horse trail from the upper end of Long Draw onto a saddle of the main ridge and thus, in half an hour, into a spring pocket on the south slope which sheltered the Fenton headquarters. Willow Creek had an air of drabness, due mostly to the neutral, weathered tone that 'dobe and timber buildings acquire after a few seasons in Texas sun and wind. But the Willow Creek yard had a look of prosperity wholly lacking at this place in the ridges. There was one square, half dug-out shack which was obviously sleeping quarters for owners and hands, alike. A make-shift feed barn and a dilapidated corral were the only other buildings. Gear and equipment were in the open and because this was a man's place and the Fentons had other chores besides the digging of a pit, there was not even an outhouse.

The effect was not of slovenliness, however. Rather it was of hard, Spartan practicality. Nothing invested in time or material which was not absolutely essential to the working of beef. This was confirmation of Steve's estimate of Hal

Fenton. The man was on a long ladder, reaching up, and he worried little about the fastenings of the rungs below him.

Hauling up at the edge of the yard, Lewellyn whistled for recognition.

The door of the shack opened almost immediately, betraying the fact that its occupants had been aware of Lewellyn's approach and had watched it. The first man out the door was about Hal Fenton's height, but a little more slight of build and aggressive of manner. This man moved with authority and sureness. The next two, sidling out to flank the first, were nondescript — mavericks without readily seen markings. Lewellyn felt a distinct disappointment when he saw the fourth man. He had hoped young Fenton had gone north with the trail herd and that he would be able to deal with the older brother. However, Randee Fenton was the last man out of the shack and Lewellyn abandoned any hope of handling this in an easy way. He swung down and moved toward the group in front of the shack.

Randee Fenton lagged behind the others. Lewellyn saw the boy was grinning wickedly, unmasked elation in his eyes. But since he remained against the wall of the shack, Steve was forced to treat first with the three riders fanned out sullenly in front of the door. These were a kind he knew. He was on sure ground. He understood how they must be handled.

"I'm Lewellyn," he said quietly, holding his

tone to a middle ground between friendliness and aggression. "A partner on Willow Creek. We've got a cut fence and some ridge stock on our grass. Anybody got an answer to that?"

The stocky man who had been first out the door glanced over his shoulder at young Fenton. Without shifting his careless position against the side of the shack, Randee nodded slightly. The stocky man spoke easily.

"I'm Sam Dreen," he said. "That was a hungry bunch of scrubs and the grass in the draw looked green to me. I didn't see any fence."

Lewellyn smiled a little. This Dreen knew his game and the cards he held. This was a checked bet. Lewellyn had not wanted to begin this with a quarrel. It reduced his chances of making a good deal for Pete with the Fentons. But he knew the cut fence would have to be settled before talk could get around to trading.

"A man needs his eyesight to live long in this country, Dreen," he suggested.

Randee Fenton pushed out from the wall, his manner still careless and confident.

"Dreen is a better man than Banta or Macambridge ever thought of being, Lewellyn —" he murmured. Steve's brows climbed a little.

"Yes — ?"

"A way of telling you that Hal isn't here to holler 'slow!' and this is a hell of a poor time to come rooting in our yard for trouble."

Lewellyn looked steadily at the boy.

"I'm old enough to know a man doesn't have

to root for trouble, Randee," he said with impact. "There's plenty, just lying around. What do you aim to do about cattle in the draw?"

Fenton glanced at Dreen. A signal appeared to pass between them. Lewellyn became conscious of the fact that the cut fence had been a trap, deliberately set for him, that this had all been carefully rehearsed. But he refused to let go of the original purpose which had brought him up into the ridges this morning.

"Nothing —" young Fenton said after a long moment, answering his question about the cattle. Lewellyn shrugged.

"Then you've seen the last of those scrubs. But let it go. Something else brought me up here."

"What?" Sam Dreen asked. Lewellyn kept his eyes on Randee Fenton and made his answer to him.

"Your brother talked about a deal with Pete and me. I'd listen, now."

"The Long Draw sections?"

"The works. The whole Willow Creek layout. With us out of the way, if you stay sober and keep your feet out of badger holes, you'll need it all, eventually."

"Crawling, Lewellyn?" Randee relished the question. Steve shook his head.

"Changing my game."

"And your proposition?"

"You and your brother are short of cash and you're trying to build up your herd as fast as you can. I think I can persuade Pete to move off of Willow Creek in a suitcase, leaving stock, equipment — everything. That would double your size, overnight. And I think we can work out a deal on payment —"

Randee Fenton glanced again at Sam Dreen and nodded agreement. A full pleasure in his own thoughts was alive in his eyes. He laughed softly.

"Sure," he said with exaggerated pleasantry. "A deal on payment is the easiest part of it. Know why, Lewellyn? Because there isn't going to be any. We're going to have Willow Creek, all right, but it isn't going to cost us any price!"

Lewellyn sensed a tightening of caution in the men facing him. Grinning recklessly, Randee Fenton continued to wind it tighter.

"Where the hell do you get off with this talk of payment, anyway, Lewellyn? You hit this country a flat-broke drifter with an iron on your leg and nothing else. Macambridge cleaned Charlie Bissel out and you cleaned out Macambridge. You think that makes you big enough to talk price to us? To hell with it!"

Fenton pushed up beside Sam Dreen.

"I've got my belly full of you and your talk, Lewellyn. Hal's on his way to the rails. When he gets back, he aims to straighten this out. But that's Hal's trouble. A little too slow. Letting the other gent drive him a little too far, first. Mixing too much patience into his planning. You're smart enough to know Lynch can't hang on to

Willow Creek against us. You wouldn't be here now, if you weren't. And you're black enough around the boot tops to know an outfit like ours, playing table stakes with nothing in its pocket, is going to stack the deck its own way. Hal's peddling our first market herd. But I've got a cut in this deal and we're going to have Willow Creek by the time he's down again from the rails."

Lewellyn eyed the four men facing him.

"I'll tell Pete that when he gets back —" he said quietly.

Randee Fenton shook his head.

"No. The sign is all down in the dust. We planned it that way. You came up here this morning to raise hell over a cut fence and some stragglers. You're not going back to the creek."

Steve watched Fenton closely, the corners of his eyes also recording the silhouettes of the others against a sudden move among them. This was the bite of the trap. And in a way, he could blame Sharon that he was in it. She had sent him out this morning with a purpose that was not him, but her. She had sent him out with desire a saddlemate and his own convictions lost in a tide of understanding he had never known before — understanding of the powerful influence one woman could exert in the life of every man.

There was a certain wry tragedy in this, for Sharon's desire had been to avoid this kind of friction and the violence which must inevitably follow it. More than a personal desire, it embraced Steve, himself, and Pete, and by

87

extension, every man on the short grass. Yet, in trying to escape it, she had sent Steve here on an errand he had realized from the beginning must almost certainly fail.

Lewellyn was conscious of his debt to Sharon, conscious of the deeply rooted strength of her convictions as to the conduct of quarrels on the *llanos,* but the fiber of pride was strongly woven in him and he knew a man who could not live with himself could not live with any woman.

"Son," he told Randee Fenton softly, "I warned you once never to prod me again!"

There was an instant of complete, motionless silence. Then the strike was made. Lewellyn realized even this had been shrewdly planned and rehearsed. Sam Dreen slapped first for his gun, forcing Lewellyn's attention to him. And as Lewellyn's attention shifted, Randee Fenton also dropped his hand for his weapon. Both of these men were fast. It was the kind of thing which could not fail, with the two flanking Fenton riders present to testify later if necessary to its legality . . . a typical range quarrel, settled with gunsmoke, proof by young Fenton that he had been in the right.

But a lot of dust had been raised above the long trail Steve Lewellyn had ridden up out of boyhood, dust which covered many recollections and masked many skills. Aware that he might possibly match Dreen but that young Fenton would have him nailed certainly, Lewellyn did not remain carefully balanced as he reached for his own gun. Instead, he flung his body forward in a bent, twisting movement. The point of his shoulder struck Sam Dreen at the ridge of his hip, just as the man fired.

Lewellyn felt the concussion of the shot, the sting of powder. With it, he heard the following jolt of Randee Fenton's gun, a shot hurried a little by his own forward drive and consequently also a little wide of its mark. Staggered by Lewellyn's lunge, Dreen lost his footing and went down. At an awkward angle, Steve slanted his gun upward under his raised left arm and fired at Fenton. Still without breaking the first startling momentum of his forward leap, he came down hard with one knee across the back of Dreen's neck, grinding the spilled man's face roughly into the dust and robbing Dreen momentarily of a chance for a second shot.

Snapping his attention back to Randee Fenton again, Steve saw the boy was still on his feet, gun in hand. He fired with more of a chance at accuracy this time and it was not until he saw his bullet spill Randee like an undercut post that he realized his first shot had been enough, that Fenton had been dying on his feet.

Dreen writhed helplessly under his knee, his gun and gun hand moved into the dirt in a search for leverage to dislodge the man above him. Lewellyn struck mercilessly at the hand with the muzzle of his own weapon and pulled Dreen's gun from his hurt fingers when they opened. Steve heaved to his feet then, his body still tense and his eyes leaping challengingly to the two Fenton hands who were to have witnessed another version of this short grass deal between neighbors.

Both men had appreciably lost interest in Lewellyn. They stood white-faced, without moving, their eyes on Randee Fenton, down on his back with blood on his belt, dead with his eyes wide open, and on Sam Dreen, now risen to his knees and spitting gravel from his crushed mouth. Lewellyn snapped an order at one of them.

"Get Dreen some water —" The rider ducked into the shack and returned with a dipper. Dreen sloshed its contents between his lips, rinsed his mouth, and spat. Dropping his own gun into its holster, Lewellyn punched the brass from Dreen's weapon and handed it back to the man. Dreen held the gun a moment, shoved it into leather, and cradled his hurt hand. He looked at Randee Fenton.

"Dead?"

The very needlessness of the question made an answer unnecessary. Dreen expected none.

"A hell of a way to do business," Dreen growled. "I told the kid that. Too risky. Now he knows what I meant."

"You've got some stock on Willow Creek grass, Dreen," Lewellyn said. "I want it back on your side of the line and our fence patched before sundown."

Dreen nodded.

"You'll get your wanting — this time, Lewellyn," he agreed. "But you know the rest of it. Hal thought a lot of that kid. He won't figure who made the mistake here. He won't take this any patient way. You smoked up any chance you ever had of making a deal with him. It'll be dog and dog, now."

"Chance — was there ever any?"

Dreen looked sharply at Lewellyn. Some innate honesty made him shake his head.

"No, I don't think so."

"Then do Fenton a favor, Dreen," Lewellyn suggested. "Tell him he'd better walk slow."

"You think I won't?" Dreen murmured. "You can be beat, but not any fast way. I've seen you work a hurry job, now. I won't forget it. Next time, I'll play my cards. And there will be a next time — !"

Lewellyn shrugged.

"It's a short ride to Willow Creek," he said. "I'll be there."

Chapter 9

A man's pride stems from many roots. Lewellyn had long cherished his own directness, but at noon he was diagonally across the Lynch ranch from the home buildings on Willow Creek and as far from them as he could possibly be without crossing the boundaries. And it was already dark when he finally loped in across the home bench, although he had accomplished nothing with which to account for the long day. Sharon saw him coming or heard him and she was at the corral when he rode up to unsaddle. This was the moment of which he had been afraid and it was fully as difficult as he had feared it would be.

In the first instant there were only three things in Sharon's eyes — relief at his return, welcome, and a woman's curiosity in the outcome of an affair in which she had a vital interest. Then this radiant simplicity dissolved, shattered into a whole array of suspicions, accusations. Steve realized his own face was betraying him as his delay in returning from the ridges had betrayed him.

Sharon did not speak. She did not come close to him. She waited until he was done with his horse, then walked up to the house with him in silence. He closed the door, unbuckled his belt, and hung it on a wall peg. She watched this with a slow tightening of her lips. Then she lit the lamp and turned toward him.

"What happened?"

Lewellyn struggled hard with the inevitable whiplash of reaction which shook a man for hours after a walk with death, a strange reversion to forgotten boyhood. An almost irresistible temptation to gild fact into a legend of bravado and personal infallibility. He spoke quietly, steadily, almost too bluntly, in his effort to let Sharon see the meeting in the Fenton yard without even the coloring it had possessed in his own eyes.

She sat opposite him at the kitchen table, her back as stiff as the back of her chair and her face slowly draining of color. She was beautiful. Not the beauty Lewellyn had seen last night in the glow of the stove at the bunk shack. Not a woman's particular beauty, even, for a man who had an impassioned belief in a thing could also look like this. A white, sharp, impersonal beauty, lighted by sub-surface fires of determination.

When his story was finished, Sharon raised her clenched hands from her lap to the top of the table. She leaned forward over them a little and she spoke carefully.

"Something inside of me keeps wanting to say that I knew this would happen, Steve. If not today, then tomorrow. It wants to keep saying that I asked too much of you, that like horses, men don't change. Maybe nothing can tear out the killer strain —"

She paused, obviously hoping she had stung him deeply enough to reach a denial. But Lewellyn said nothing. She had heard him out without interruption. He had to hear her.

"— But that isn't fair, Steve," she went on reluctantly. "I know it isn't. And I want to be fair. I want it terribly. I don't understand, but maybe once in his life a man is crowded into a corner from which there is no way out. Maybe that's where you were, today. You went up onto the ridges to do what I asked you, to find us all a way out of the *llanos* . . . without trouble. I'm remembering that. I'll pack for you. Get out of here tonight. Ride north, Steve. Write me when you've found a place where we can live the way I've asked you to try. By the time your letter gets here, Pete will be back and we'll have made some kind of a deal with Hal Fenton."

Lewellyn put the fingers of one hand down hard on the table cloth in front of him. He looked at the square, blunt nails, the heavy cording rooting each finger. And he looked at Sharon's hands, brown as his own, but without scars; slender and long of finger, sensitive, but with only a fraction of the physical strength of his. Different hands and a different way of thinking.

The results, he knew, if he left the *llanos* now, were inevitable. Sam Dreen, sullenly waiting his employer's return at the place on the ridges, would think his parting threat had taken root.

94

His thinking would go beyond this. He would think that Steve Lewellyn believed the Willow Creek ranch had no chance of standing against Fenton. He would draw this conclusion, also, from Lewellyn's departure. And this conclusion would strengthen his confidence; it would strengthen Fenton's confidence. Where there had once been a willingness to pay a fair price for the Long Draw sections, there would now be a belief that all Willow Creek could be had virtually for nothing if the pressure was built high enough.

And there was Pete to consider. Because he was old and because of Sharon, Pete would swallow a lot, but he had been too long on the *llanos* to lie quietly while a neighbor rolled him off his land. These were the things Sharon did not see. Or if she saw them, she refused them their proper importance. These were the things which bound Steve more tightly to Willow Creek than he had been bound before, so long as he still owned affection for Pete and a hope that time might make Sharon understand that a man who dealt in death was not always a killer.

He looked up and spoke, a desire to be gentle making his voice a little unsteady.

"I can't go tonight, Sharon. I would if I could, since you've asked me — since you say you'll follow when I write. But there isn't any easy way out of this. I've got to stay until it's through —"

"Until you're brought home to me dead, this time — or until they've buried Hal Fenton, up on the ridges. Is that it?"

"It might work either way. We can hope it doesn't. But we'll have to see and I'll have to stay until Fenton has pulled in his horns or he's paid Pete a fair price for Willow Creek."

Sharon rose. The color began flooding back into her cheeks.

"You've made a fool of me, Steve," she said bitterly. "Life is a big thing to me and I've wanted a big man — as big as you. You lay in my bed and I took care of you until you were well enough to leave it. You used stolen money to buy in with dad, so that I saw you every day for months. You laughed at me and listened to me, by turn, until you had me believing you could see my kind of life. And now, after last night, after you're sure, you tell me you'll have no more of doing what I ask."

She paused, looking at him steadily.

"Understand this, Steve, I don't care what kind of price dad gets for Willow Creek. It's enough to me if he gets rid of it. I want to get off the *llanos*. I wanted to go with you. I'll never want to go with another man as much. But I want order and a town. I want to grow with it. And I'll have it. Last night bound me to nothing."

"No," Lewellyn agreed softly. "I think the rope dropped on me, not on you."

"If it did, you cut it cleanly enough on the ridge, today," Sharon answered. "I love you, Steve, if it means anything now. I think you loved me. But it's over, now — done. If there's loss, it's mine. There's nothing to keep you here. Nothing at all. I'll make Pete see that. If you stay you'll only bring trouble, here in the house and out on the grass. Trouble Pete is too old to face. We existed before you came; we can do it again, Pete and me. Move on, Steve —"

"North?"

"Where you want," Sharon replied quietly. "I said it was over. I meant that. I want a man who has some other pride than his hardness toward others and respect for a higher authority than his fists and his gun!"

Lewellyn rose and crossed to the wall peg. He looked soberly across at the girl as he pulled on his belt.

"I hope we're not making a mistake, Sharon —"

The girl shook her head with conviction.

"We've already made our mistakes — both of us. This is to keep us from making more."

Lewellyn pulled open the door. A sudden, sharp struggle sawed at him, its violence increased by a momentary softening in Sharon's eyes. He stood framed in the opening, aware that a step inward, a little contrition, and fresh promises could bridge all of the unpleasantness of the hour past. But he also knew that this would only be delaying the inevitable, that tonight would recur again. Sharon would not change. He could not. And there was too much pain involved for repetition. He stepped across the threshold.

From the outside, he said:

"If you find that man — the one that suits you, Sharon — I'd like to see him sometime —"

And he pulled the door closed.

It was nearly midnight when Lewellyn rode into the Fenton yard again. He did not dismount. A rangy dog was about the place, his uproar a sufficient call for attention. Someone within the shack growled a sleepy challenge.

"It's Lewellyn," Steve called. "Send Dreen out. I want to see him."

Imprecations sounded inside. A lamp was lit. Dreen came out after a moment in pants and undershirt. He brought the lamp with him.

"What the hell is chewing on you now, Lewellyn?" he grunted angrily.

"We've got to have a little understanding, Dreen."

"On what? We settled all that this morning."

"Not this. I'm pulling out."

"Oh — ?" Dreen was silent for a moment. "That makes things easier."

"Some," Lewellyn agreed. "Fenton can make a better deal with Pete Lynch and his girl than he ever could with me. What we've got to understand, what Fenton has got to understand when he gets back, is that there does have to be some kind of a deal. I'm assigning my share in Willow Creek to a man who'll go a long ways toward seeing Lynch gets a fair something — that he at least gets a chance to sell. And if that doesn't

98

work, I won't be so far away I can't be reached. I'm finished here, Dreen. I don't want to come back. But I will if I have to."

Dreen nodded.

"I'll tell Hal," he said.

"You'll do better than that," Lewellyn corrected quietly. "You'll make him see I mean this. I don't expect him to make Pete rich, I just want it to be a square deal. If it isn't, I'll hunt him down and I'll hunt you down. Understand?"

Dreen nodded again.

"I'm no fool, Lewellyn. This ought to suit Hal. You worried him. Old man Lynch never did. There'll be a deal offered on Willow Creek, I think. A clean one. Hal can use the grass, and at a decent price, if he can pay for it as he can. You're making a good move, Lewellyn. You're saving a lot of trouble for all of us. Hal knows what he's building here. He was afraid you were trying to build the same thing. With you gone, he's not apt to be too ringy."

"I figured that," Lewellyn said shortly. "See to it I didn't figure wrong!"

Reining his horse about, Lewellyn rode briskly out of the yard.

Steve was asleep on the walk in front of the Texas Pride saloon in La Mesa, sitting with his back against the weathered wall of the building, when Charlie Bissel opened his front door in the morning. The creak of the hinges and Bissel's soft oath roused him. When he opened his eyes,

Bissel was standing in the doorway, his eyes running over the bedroll and gear lashed behind Steve's saddle on the horse at the rack. While Bissel completed his inspection, Steve rose and stretched. The saloonman turned toward him.

"Looking for me?"

Steve nodded.

"You're Lewellyn, from out at the Lynch place, aren't you?"

Steve nodded again. Bissel turned toward the interior of the saloon.

"Come in and drag up a chair. I was just fixing breakfast," he offered.

Lewellyn followed him across the dark, stuffy public room and into the quarters at the rear. These were neat, orderly, clean, and a good breakfast smell was in the air. Lewellyn found a wash basin, soap, a towel, and scrubbed the night from his face and hands. Bissel put the meal onto the table and sat down opposite him. They ate in silence. When they had finished, Bissel leaned back and methodically rolled himself a tight, smooth cigarette. He looked up as he lit it.

"Pulling out, eh?" he asked matter-of-factly. "Why?"

Lewellyn considered his answer and decided masking the truth was pointless.

"Orders."

"From Pete?"

"No."

"The girl, then." Bissel grinned. "A woman

can raise hell. Where you going?"

"North," Lewellyn said. "Maybe Kansas. Figured I might drag off of the *llanos* for a while. Maybe try a piece of the railroad land the government is peddling up there."

Bissel's sharp eyes probed.

"Man, you're hit bad!" he commented. "I've heard Sharon Lynch say her piece before, but I never thought I'd see a whang-leather Texan take holt of that bit!"

"Might be several things you haven't seen," Lewellyn suggested drily.

"Such as — ?"

"This —" Lewellyn drew a folded square of note paper from his breast pocket, snapped it open, and tossed it down in front of the saloonman. Bissel studied its contents. Finally he raised his head with a curious expression in his eyes.

"An assignment to your half of Pete's ranch — to me. Why?"

"Two reasons," Lewellyn said. "In the first place, I never owned that half of Pete's ranch. He split Willow Creek because I handed him a pouch of money. That pouch came out of Les Macambridge's shirt and what was in it came out of your safe."

"Pete knew that when he used it?"

"Probably. But I never told him so. Just that I hadn't robbed you."

"I always figured Macambridge did it. One of the women finally admitted he had been in town.

I figured he got Banta, too. But it was hard to fit you in and the whole deal was a tough thing to prove. I've had plenty of time to wait, and now it's paid off. You said you had two reasons for chucking this assignment at me. What's the other?"

"Sharon is going to move Pete as soon as he's back from his drive to the rails. She's going to squeeze him into selling out, with Hal Fenton the only buyer in sight. I came through the ridges on my way in here last night. I did what I could to see he gets a smooth deal. But that isn't enough. Not with Fenton. You're a good trader and it's going to take a damned good man in a trade to get Pete off Willow Creek with anything more than his skin."

Bissel folded the assignment and put it into a pocket. "Pete will make out all right, Lewellyn," he said quietly. "Now I'm going to tell you something. I'm fed up here, myself. I've got a buyer for this place coming up from Mexico. I'm going north, too. But I'm one up on you. I've got my place picked out. You've got no strings on you and I like the way you do business. Supposing you take on a chore for me?"

Lewellyn shrugged.

"Why not?"

"There's a town up in Kansas called Brokenbow. Three shacks and a spittoon, now, likely. But it's on the rail survey and far enough out now from the railroad for a man to buy in before the boom hits. Once the rails reach it, it'll become a shipping center for Texas beef until the railroad moves on out to another town closer to us, here. And while the drovers are shipping from it, it'll be a real heller for business. That's why I've picked it — that and the fact that it lies in good country and should live on pretty husky after the railroad has passed it by. I've been writing a mess of letters to a hardware man up there. Fellow by the name of Jed Barnage."

"That's got something to do with me?"

Bissel nodded.

"Plenty. That's the chore. Barnage has agreed to throw me up a building and equip it. I told you I liked the way you do business —" Bissel tapped the pocket containing Lewellyn's assignment. "— I want you to take a pocketful of my cash north to Brokenbow and see that I get my money's worth in that building. It would be worth a solid commission to me, and it would give you some income while you're getting a piece of that government ground squared around so it'll feed you."

Lewellyn considered the offer. Bissel had solved his most serious problem in riding north — a temporary income while he was getting located. And one Kansas town was the same as another, as far as he was concerned. Brokenbow would do as well as the next. He was not deceived by Bissel's approval of his way of doing business. There was honesty involved in the assignment of his half of Willow Creek to Bissel. His offer, Steve was convinced, was only half gratitude for this. The other half lay behind Bissel's careful measurement of the hang of his gun and the cut of his face.

"Maybe I'm a little too sudden for a carpenter boss, Bissel," Lewellyn said quietly. "That stop I made last night in the ridges was the second in twenty-four hours. I got in a little jam up there yesterday morning. They buried the Fenton kid last night."

"A man in a saloon hears things," Bissel said imperturbably. "His carcass wasn't even stiff before I heard that little sidewinder had finally gotten his. What's the odds in that? You're going north to change your stripes, aren't you? I get that idea, anyhow. To make a try of some kind at plowing the kind of a furrow Pete's girl has been selling you. So you'll be a different critter in Brokenbow than you are here."

Lewellyn winced at the man's penetration, but he grinned.

"All right," he agreed. "It's Brokenbow, then. But one thing — nobody knows where I've gone."

Bissel frowned.

"Nothing's ever that final, Lewellyn," he protested. "It's a mistake to make it so, deliberately. Sharon Lynch is an almighty fine woman this minute, and there's a lot of growing in her, yet. On the short grass, we're bred to appetites, strong ones, man and woman, both. If she loses touch with you, she'll find herself another. It's in the blood. And you're the kind who should have a woman like her."

Lewellyn shook his head and rose from the table.

"Not now, I'm not. Maybe sometime —" He shrugged. "Look, I want to be moving —"

Bissel kicked back his chair.

"You can start in an hour."

"And where I'm going — ?"

"I'll help you be a fool, since you want it that way. If I'm asked, I won't know where the hell you are —"

BOOK TWO

Chapter 1

It is hard to know what a man wants, if it can be known at all. In the beginning, comfort; something to eat when hunger growls and a place to sleep out of the wind. The security of infancy. A little later the desire is to be like someone grown. A father, perhaps. Or an uncle. Or a moonshiner in the brush with a scar on his cheek and a deep bell voice and a stock of scary stories and time to tell them. Boyhood dreaming. And then an end to dreams. A restless desire for escape from monotony. New hills. New faces. Independence. A woman, sometime, and finally permanence. A long ride, too often in a circle.

Lewellyn dismounted at a rack on the main street of Brokenbow with a strong feeling of impotence, of having wrestled with himself in the dark. In the three years since he had ridden out of La Mesa, there had been accomplishment. This had been inevitable. Time and the wind were always in motion. The Kansas Pacific had reached Brokenbow. A muddy, rutted wagon track had become a street. Buildings had risen. Among them was Charlie Bissel's U. S.

Grant saloon, which Steve had built for him at a fraction of its present value. So, also, the newspaper plant across the street and Jed Barnage's new store and the loading pens below the tracks. These were the mechanics of a net which had closed in on Steve Lewellyn.

Bissel was in the Grant, now, a businessman. A Kansan with the *llanos* far behind him, apparently forgotten. Bissel was flexible. He wore his new coat well. There were others who adjusted easily. John Devore, the printer, who had come in from Abilene with his type cases, his press, his wife, and with his tail between his legs. Devore fitted the street assiduously. He was dry in dry weather and wet when it rained. When there was mud on his boots he wiped them clean; to hell with filling up the chuck-hole into which he had stepped. He edited his news with a kind of desperation which succeeded in making him no enemies, but which could not make him friends.

Lewellyn did not know for certain — he had never made a point of it with Bissel — but he thought it was the saloonman who had brought Sharon Lynch to Brokenbow. Quite possibly because Charlie could see Steve's restlessness and perhaps because he fathomed Sharon's unhappiness. Maybe with an idea that an old mistake could be healed. If this was so, Bissel was a fool. Rivers do not run backward. Time does not run backward. And now Sharon was married to the printer from Abilene.

Steve had not inquired, but there was little

that was secret in Brokenbow. Pete Lynch had gotten something for his place on Willow Creek. A third of its value. Bissel had thought it was fair, under the circumstances. Steve thought it was fair. Pete had gone to Abilene with his daughter. But Pete had left all that he had built on the *llanos*. He could not stand the separation. Abilene had been too small. It had been too unfamiliar. And Pete had not had the narcotic of work for his hands. Pete had been dead for over two years.

Sharon had been married to Devore nearly as long. And now she was in Brokenbow.

Perhaps Bissel had written to Abilene that opportunity was out here. A need for a paper, even one which was opposition to neither God nor man. Or something bigger than Bissel, working without plan and with far more bitter irony, could have brought Sharon out with the rails. So now she was on this street and Steve Lewellyn was on a homestead section up the valley and cattle were coming into the loading pens on the railroad. Cattle from the biggest drover's outfit on the *llanos*. Cattle wearing one of Hal Fenton's brands. This was a different place and a different time. But nothing else had changed — except Steve Lewellyn.

Steve stepped up onto the yellow, little-worn planking of the walk. Small eddies of dead wind stirred dust from pockets along the street. A trotting dog veered a little and barked disinterest-

108

edly at him, swinging its attention in a moment to a farm wagon loaded with children at the rail before the post office. For eighty yards along whisky row, the racks were crowded with horses wearing Texas brands. Charlie Bissel had competition. Willow Creek Ranch had expanded to cover a third of the county, down on the *llanos*, and Fenton ran big crews. Night was coming in off the grass. Beyond the high end of the street, on the slope of the low ridge back of town, the supper fires of Fenton's trail-herd camp were dying down.

Ord Keown, turned out in a fresh shirt and a carefully brushed coat for his night rounds, came out of the Grant and moved toward Steve. The low red sun beyond the ridge made a bright spot of the marshal's badge on Keown's lapel.

" 'Evening, farmer," Keown said. It was almost a ritual. Ord seemed to find amusement in the stain of loam and sand under Steve's nails. Incredulity too, perhaps, but amusement. And he invariably used the same mocking salutation. Steve nodded without expression, taking obstinate pleasure in passing by the edge of the marshal's greeting as coolly as the man offered it. Keown chuckled thinly and would have swung on but Lewellyn arrested him with a movement of his hand.

"Stick around, Ord —" he suggested. Keown ran long-lashed, impersonal eyes over him.

He shook his head.

"No, I'm busy, tonight."

Lewellyn accepted both the refusal and its curtness with a prodding of maliciousness. The marshal would be busier, directly. He watched Ord go on up the walk with an easy stride, small and tailored and well aware of the respect men held for his kind. Lethal, virile, and vain, without pretense at any of the three. The law of Brokenbow.

When Keown was gone, Lewellyn stepped into the Grant, moving midway down the bar to the section Charlie Bissel tended. The Grant was busy, crowded with townsmen and an overflow of Texans who had not been able to find room or service at the Wagon Wheel or the Spur, both a few doors up the street. Bissel's apron was smudged and he looked tired.

"A Roanoke, Charlie," Lewellyn told him. Bissel hooked the bottle off the backbar, drew its cork, and set it down beside a finger glass.

"I didn't look for you in for a day or two, Steve," he said. "The drovers won't start pulling out till tomorrow or the next day."

Lewellyn poured a drink and swallowed it. He rang the glass back down on the bar.

"I'm looking for Fenton. Has he been in here this afternoon?"

Charlie Bissel's thick brows drew down across his eyes. He poured another drink into Lewellyn's glass and set out a glass for himself.

"Hal's half drunk," he said carefully. "Most of his crew's gone the whole way. Hal got his money on his last herd today and he's paid his boys off. Every jack of them is smoking hot tonight. And they're getting wise to the fact this town don't love 'em. Look, Steve, you're homesteading, now. You're a hell of a long way from Willow Creek. It's taken you three years to get where you are. You've got no truck with trail herds. You're forgetting that."

"No," Lewellyn said. "I'll do nothing a farmer wouldn't, but I'll do as much as any farmer would. I want to see Fenton."

Charlie Bissel shrugged, something almost mocking in his eyes as though he too saw something incredulous in Steve's grim attachment to the sod of his homestead.

"Just so you remember, Steve," he agreed. "Hal was at the Spur half an hour ago. There's been a game on. I don't think it's broken up. But maybe you ought to wait, Steve. Better wait till tomorrow. Tonight Brokenbow is out of Kansas. Tonight it's down on the *llanos* — with the lid pried off. You don't want trouble —"

"No —" Lewellyn agreed without commitment. He put a coin down on the bar. Bissel slid the silver into his till. His voice dropped, reaching out to put a friend's caution on the earthstained man before him.

"There are some men that trouble just follows, Steve. I'd remember that. You're one of them —"

Lewellyn stepped away from the bar.

"I've forgotten nothing, Charlie," he said quietly. "Nothing. If Ord Keown ducks in here again, you'd better send him along up to the Spur."

Lewellyn quit the Grant unhurriedly. He paused on the walk outside to finish a cigarette and to watch the sun die. Brokenbow was without paint, without color or softness, but in these changing moments between day and night it was touched with both so that a man could see beauty where there was none. Steve wondered if this wasn't the root of the mistake Sharon had made on the *llanos* — that she still might be making now. He wondered if she could really see what a town like this was — if she could see the people which made it for looking at the town itself. He thought it likely she couldn't. Not the people and not the frictions which kindled trouble.

Across the street Ruth Barnage had stopped beside the wagon loaded with kids in front of the post office. A man and a woman were on the seat now, listening to what Jed Barnage's wife knew of the comings and goings in Brokenbow. Lewellyn decided the family in the wagon was the Westfalls, homesteaders from Tie Creek. His smoke done, he sailed his cigarette into the street and moved on up the walk. As he passed in front of Cragar's store, which lay between the Grant and the Spur, Zoe Barnage came down the steps. She stopped on the next-to-the-bottom tread, so that her head was as high as Lewellyn's, and the bold, quick smile in her eyes ran down across her lips.

There was warm red life and an awareness of it in Zoe Barnage. Too much of it for her to keep contained. She swung the balance of her body deliberately so that a breath of the wind blew her dress revealingly against her. She was all woman and proud of it. Steve had seen her sporadically since he had come to Brokenbow. Restlessness. A periodic thing. Like a trip in to a barber or a session with a bottle at one of the saloons. Something a man had to get out of him — or an answer to a craving. Companionship. He had gotten no more from Zoe. He had asked for nothing more. But what she had given, she had given freely and with a relish in participation. Steve liked her. He liked her pride in her aliveness and her womanhood. He liked the absence of false restraints in her. He admired her judgment of values. In Brokenbow, where there was constant talk of ordinances and curfews and survey lines — the restrictions with which men hampered themselves when they gathered together in one place — it was good to savor Zoe's freedom. Steve doubted if she wore more than one petticoat. To some she was probably a hussy. Likely she was a rebel. And she sure as hell was unconventional. Steve grinned at her.

"Hello," she said. Her challenge touched even her voice. "Been by the house?"

"I just rode in," Lewellyn answered. "Some business."

"At the Grant or the Spur or the Wagon Wheel — or maybe the *Courier* office!"

Steve glanced across the street at the building housing John Devore's paper. He frowned a little. He wondered if Bissel was responsible for this also. Sharon would have been as tactiturn about their former relationship as he had himself been. She had made an effort equal to his own to avoid him since she had come in over the rails with her husband. Yet Zoe had some knowledge that they had known each other; and Steve was reluctant to believe either John Devore's wife or himself had betrayed anything which would be apparent to the superficial kind of observation of which Zoe was capable.

Zoe waited for a moment. When he did not answer, she laughed and stepped down past him.

"Stop by," she said. "There'll be a moon up when your business is done. You could do with a moon, Steve Lewellyn!"

She crossed the walk and moved into the street, her skirt swinging with a touch of exaggeration as she angled toward the wagon where her mother still talked with the Westfalls. Once she looked back, invitation still plain in her eyes. Lewellyn replaced his hat and swung forward. As he did so, light blossomed in the windows of the newspaper office opposite, throwing the name of the *Courier* into relief on the glass. Lewellyn could see John Devore, bent over a high table; and back of him, Sharon. He drew up again for a moment, waiting without real reason. Sharon crossed behind her husband and stopped against the window.

Lewellyn's hand went to his hat, bending the brim in a half lift. With the light behind her and dusk settling rapidly along the street, it was possible Sharon did not see him. He didn't know. He dropped his hand with a queer little sag of spirit. He recognized the cause. A self-imposed hurt, this occasional thinking of Willow Creek, and with its own strange kind of satisfaction. He would have given much to know if there was a breath of hurt still in Sharon, but he well knew the knowledge could have little real value. This desire, which was not dead, he kept locked with others within him, where it could not escape him. As Sharon turned back from the window Lewellyn shouldered through the door of the Spur.

This was the latest building along Whisky Row. A specialized palace, built with Texas money for the trailherd trade. The farmers slowly filling the tillable sections surrounding the town and the better class of townspeople avoided the Spur. Part of this was because Sid Lowell's prices were high, his games no-limit, and a man could be badly burned between breaths in Lowell's place if he had too much whisky in him. Part of it was because Lowell had brought in girls from the river towns to help build his trade and these were the first of their kind in Brokenbow. But mostly it was because when the rails came, and after them the Texas herds driving north for shipment, a line had grown up in Brokenbow as it had in other

Kansas rail towns between things connected with the drovers and things connected with the land and the backcountry which had originally brought the town to life. A line slow in being drawn, but sharply dividing and being continually stretched closer to the point of rupture.

The Spur was in two parts, one separated from the other by the pillars of an open partition. On one side, a long bar faced a tawdry little stage. Between stage and bar was an open area of poorly kept floor, ringed by small wirework tables and chairs to match. It was into this section of the smoky hall the street door opened. The other section, beyond the pillars, held the wheels, the tables, and the dice cages. The Spur represented a large investment, as saloons went, but Lowell had been shrewd enough to use his money to buy size and space, not elegance and atmosphere. To a Texan at the end of a dusty drive, the accessibility and supply of a thing far outweighed its quality. A universal trait.

The bar section of the Spur was virtually deserted when Lewellyn entered. The whole traffic of the place was jammed into the other room. Attention was focused on a big, felted poker table in its center. A game was in progress. Likely the one Bissel had mentioned. A big one. Lewellyn passed between the pillars and put the point of his shoulder against the thin edge of the crowd. He was big and his weight was high on him, so that there was force in the swing of his shoulders. He moved steadily, working to within a pair of yards of the table. Close enough to see the players and the play.

Five men were seated around the felt. Hal Fenton, Sid Lowell, one of Sid's house men, a drover from Fenton's crew, and Socrates McKenna. Fenton was apparently playing in thin luck. His drover seemed to be riding the same horse. Sid and his man — professionals — would be covering, only sitting in to keep a hot and profitable game going. Doc McKenna, gnomelike among bigger men and looking like a red-bearded, flame-horned owl, sat with his arms thrust out in front of him around a disorderly welter of chips worth a good man's pay for a year.

Lewellyn watched a hand open cautiously on white chips. They turned red in the first round and McKenna jumped them to blue, refused his draw, and sat unblinkingly behind the five cards dealt to him. In swift succession Lowell, his dealer, and the drover let go. Hal Fenton, obviously a little drunk and with his mouth strained and tight, scowled blackly across the table, attempting to measure Brokenbow's medical man.

Lewellyn studied the face of the boss of Willow Creek. There seemed little change since the distant day they had met in the draw above Pete Lynch's place. Time had left no appreciable mark. Neither had responsibility and the weight heaped onto Fenton by the amazing, ruthless growth of his ranch and his holdings. Watching the man reach for a decision now, Lewellyn knew how Fenton worked, how he would always work. He looked for the sure thing. He measured his own cards. When he went ahead, it was with reasonable surety he could not be checked. Poker, Steve thought, must be an agony to a man so built and so deliberate. Luck was something on which he could not by nature rely. Force, strength, intimidation, power — these things, yes — if they provided a sure route to an objective. But not luck.

Fenton's decision came slowly. It was a hard wait for every man in the room. A gaunt new Swede farmer from the back country, standing in front of Lewellyn, began to sweat. Moisture on the back of his neck stained the frayed rim of his collar. With a sudden movement, the Swede bit away half of the plug of tobacco in his hand.

"God!" he muttered under his breath. He began to chew strongly.

Hal Fenton raised his eyes slowly from his cards. He looked at the little man across the table from him.

"You're bluffing, McKenna," he said with studied conviction. He thrust out a stack of chips to match the heap the doctor had on offer. Men close to the table gasped. This was a killing bet. The sound of sharply drawn breaths ran through the room. The Swede farmer in front of Steve stopped chewing.

"God!" he said again.

Doc McKenna fanned his cards down. He

grinned across the table.

"A man can't bluff every time, Fenton," he said. "I've got 'em this time."

Hal Fenton came slowly to his feet, his lips bloodless and his eyes on the mass of chips in front of the little doctor.

"We'll have another round later," he said shortly. "Nothing ever ends this way, Doc!"

Sock McKenna leaned across the table and dragged the last pot toward him. He rocked his head up side-wise.

"Any time, Fenton," he said agreeably. "Any time at all."

The broad, untroubled smile which wrinkled McKenna's rawboned Scottish face in no way drew the enmity from this exchange. Fenton jerked his hat down on his head and turned away from the table. His eyes touched Lewellyn and held. Steve nodded slightly.

"I've been looking for you, Hal," he said evenly. The Swedish farmer saw Lewellyn's face and stumbled hurriedly out of the path which suddenly wedged open between Hal Fenton and Steve. Fenton rocked a little on widely planted feet. The flood of his tightly held anger churned swiftly from Doc McKenna to Lewellyn.

Chapter 2

Steve waited a moment, meeting Fenton's angry stare, then spoke again, putting his words down flatly in the sudden silence of the room.

"I want to talk to you, Hal —"

Fenton's head jerked. "Commence!" he snapped.

Lewellyn took an easy step forward, leaving no room for a man to come between Fenton and himself.

"A section of your herd went through my fence last night. I warned you about them when you bedded it down so close to me. I told you to keep them to open land and away from my line."

A man jostled through the crowd past Lewellyn's elbow and stopped a yard to one side of him. Turning his head a little, Steve caught Ord Keown's metallic, non-committal stare. Fenton, also, looked at Ord. Something he saw in the marshal's eyes seemed to steady him.

"A herd gaunted by a long drive is hard to keep from water, Lewellyn," he said. "And I'm shipping no beef out of Brokenbow till it's watered and fattened after the drive. Next time you file a homestead, keep out of the bottoms. Leave grass and water where cattle can get to them. A fence ain't a farm, ain't a crop. And you're no farmer.

You've stood no loss. It might happen again. Then what?"

"It won't happen again, Hal," Lewellyn answered quietly. "I warned you. Now I'll have my due or I'll hurt."

Doc McKenna had moved to the cash cage at the lower end of the room. The chatter of his chips falling into the rack on the counter's stick and the clink of silver passing across to him came plainly up the room. The silence held for a long moment, except for this sound. Then the crowd began to stir with the movement of Fenton's men starting in radially toward the big center table. They moved surely, unhurried. The drover who had been in the big game with his boss turned quarteringly beside Fenton and shoved forward. Fenton remained motionless, waiting. Lewellyn watched the room, seeing the initial impact of his blunt demand fade as the trail crew closed in on him.

He glanced appealingly at Keown. Ord's metallic stare did not change. The man was astraddle the fence.

He intended to remain there, for now. Steve discounted him and measured the others. Moving fast but deliberately, Lewellyn drove a shoulder against Fenton's advancing table-mate. The man wheeled full around under the impact, staggering off-balance against the Swedish homesteader. As the fellow spun, Lewellyn lifted the gun from under the raised tail of his coat. Sight of the weapon jarred Fenton.

121

He lunged forward. Lewellyn reversed himself and stepped aside. As Fenton shot past him, he drew the barrel of the weapon in his hand sharply along the side of Fenton's head.

The timing was clean. Fenton sagged. Lewellyn caught him, jerked him around, and stabbed the muzzle of the gun deep into the muscles of Fenton's back. The man fought momentary slackness from his knees and drew himself erect with a slow shake of his head. But he was careful under the pressure of the gun. The rest of the crew, sensing a reversal but being unable to identify it because of the partial screening of those about the table by the nervous, silent crowd, eased their pressure. Lewellyn spoke softly at the back of Fenton's head.

"Fifty dollars, Hal," he said. "That fence cost me fifty dollars. It costs less to bury a man in Brokenbow!"

Fenton tried to turn his head over his shoulder. Lewellyn leaned forward a fraction of an inch, increasing the pressure of the gun muzzle. Slowly — slowly enough that every man in the Spur could see that this was a beginning, not an end — Fenton reached out a thin roll of bills from a breast pocket. Handling them awkwardly, he folded several of them together and held them up under his ear. Lewellyn lifted them out of his fingers, thrust them carelessly into a jacket pocket, and stepped back.

"We're square, Hal," he said. "Thanks —"

Fenton turned.

"You should have let me forget you, Lewellyn," he said softly. "I'm busy enough. I think I could have. I think I could have forgotten everything. But not now. You've got too fast a gun in my book for Brokenbow."

Lewellyn shook his head.

"You're remembering somebody else, Hal," he said. He smiled a little. "This isn't my gun. I just borrowed it from one of your boys. All I've got is a homestead section and a string of fence. That's all. I'm a farmer."

"Yeah, fence," Fenton said. "We never did agree on fences, Lewellyn. Some day you're going to string one too many!"

Steve's smile did not change. He started backing carefully through the open lane between himself and the door. Beside this lane, close to the pillars dividing the Spur, two of Fenton's men stood. One of these thrust out a foot to trip Lewellyn as he approached. Steve heard the movement, sensed its purpose, and lengthened one backward-reaching stride so that the sharp heel of his boot came down on the instep of the outstretched foot. The man swore softly and his face sharpened with pain, but he made no other move.

A freshened wind had come up along the street. It touched Lewellyn as he reached the doors. A man was waiting on the walk before the Spur, carefully clear of the awning so that the strong light of a low moon revealed him plainly.

Lewellyn flung a taut glance at him, saw that the man wanted to talk, and turned down the walk with invitation in the slight cant of his head. The man turned and fell in beside him.

"Well, McKenna?" Steve asked. Doc McKenna laughed. It was a round sound, with honesty, and suddenly easing after the tension within the Spur.

"Never seen a Texan take an honest-to-God bite out of another one before," McKenna said. "Your chew taste as good as mine?" He slapped at a pocket weighted down with winnings.

"I wasn't biting for fun!" Lewellyn answered. McKenna's laugh died.

"Neither was I! Look, we don't like the same people. How about adding up our grouches over a couple of shot-glasses?"

Talk was a mood with Lewellyn. He didn't want it, now. He shook his head.

"Later," he said.

"Sure —" Sock McKenna shrugged with good humor. He laughed again, softly. "Sure. I'll be around anytime. But will you, Lewellyn? How much prodding is Hal Fenton going to take from a homesteader?"

Still chuckling a little, McKenna pulled up and turned back. Lewellyn continued on up the walk. The doctor's casualness was not deceptive. Neither was his laughter. There was grimness to both. McKenna knew where he stood. He knew where all of Brokenbow stood. McKenna did not like Texans. He did not like their cattle. He did not like what the shipping of *llanos* beef was doing to his town — what it would continue to do. And he said so, often and bluntly.

He was outspoken in his opposition to the Fenton crews when much of the town was still only grumbling. He knew the need for unity and for strength if Fenton's crews were to be matched and checked. He even knew the kind of men who could match and check the Texans. So this had been a bid for Steve Lewellyn. A bid based on the friction between Steve and Hal Fenton in the Spur. A carelessly masked hope that Lewellyn would swing with the town — with McKenna.

Steve had respect for the little doctor. McKenna had wisdom and sharp understanding of the dangers to a rail town inherent in its shipping pens. Drovers needed grass — Kansas grass — to fatten their stock after the long and often dry drive up from the *llanos*. They needed it close to the town from which they were to ship. The drovers were not lawless. There was no more deviltry in them than in Missourians or river crews or like kinds. But they were determined. And their interests were prime interests, always. If they broke up the small farms about a shipping center in order to get the grass they needed, they would lose no sleep. There were many among them who believed turned sod was an offense against their private god. A sincere enough belief. And none of them could see that a town needed farms in which to sink its roots. None of them saw far enough ahead to realize that when the rails had built further westward they would make their drives to shipping points closer to their home range. They did not see that Brokenbow had to defend its farms to exist after the drovers were gone. Or if they saw, they didn't give a damn. They were stockmen. To hell with farms.

So this was the real danger. This was the danger Doc McKenna saw. Not the Texans themselves. Not their drunkenness. Not the blandishments Sid Lowell and others had introduced to secure their trade. Ord Keown's problem of maintaining orderliness on the streets was more spectacular. It was noisier. It had a certain color which made the doings of the day, the boisterous rowdyism, and the women in the Spur subject to concern and table talk in most of the houses in town. But McKenna and maybe Jed Barnage and a few others saw which side of the blade was edged and they were gathering their forces.

They wanted Steve Lewellyn. He knew why. He had known since the day the construction trains of the Kansas Pacific smoked in off the prairie and it became inevitable that some *llanos* outfit would drive to Brokenbow for shipment. Maybe it had been Charlie Bissel again who had helped build the legend. Maybe it had been something in Lewellyn's own aloofness, his walk, his eyes. But Brokenbow knew that Steve

Lewellyn was a hard man, able, and swift in his judgments of right and wrong. As the history of his gun had made Ord Keown marshal of Brokenbow, the history of his own gun had made Steve Lewellyn a man sought after and catered to by those who had built the town and dreamed its dreams of permanence.

What Bissel had not hinted to the town and what McKenna and the others could not see was something which was buried deep in Lewellyn. Something which had been planted on Willow Creek. Something which had made him tie himself to a plot of ground too small to run stock. Something which had made Kansas a new beginning for him. Something with which there could be no compromise. A determination to trade for peace. The principle which Sharon Lynch had preached on the *llanos*. The gulf between Sharon and himself was not narrowed by her presence now in Brokenbow, and this determination was the one bridge which still bound Lewellyn to her. It was something he would not relinquish.

Opposite the *Courier* office, Lewellyn pulled up on the walk and stood motionless. He had tried to believe that the railroad meant nothing. He had tried to believe he could hold himself apart from Fenton and his men. Yet now he knew what he had known from the beginning, that he could not do this. His acceptance of Sharon's principles was in itself a compromise. He would trade for the rights of others. He could do that. But his own rights were closer to him than even Sharon had been. And his plot of land was the source of those rights. An eddy was spinning. He could not stay in it and avoid the vortex. With a decisive snap of his cigarette into the gutter he stepped down from the walk and strode briskly across the street toward the lighted windows of the newspaper office.

Chapter 3

Preoccupied, absorbed in his sudden decision and the way out it offered, Lewellyn stepped into the office of the *Brokenbow Courier.* Only Devore was behind the counter. Sharon had, Steve thought, gone into the living quarters in the rear of the building. Devore looked up irritably from his composing table and offered no greeting. Lewellyn pushed the door closed behind him and crossed to the counter bisecting the office.

"You're working late, John," he suggested. "Where's Sharon?"

Devore slid slowly from his stool and took off his glasses. With the typesetter's hump gone from his shoulders and his feet planted solidly on the floor Devore was a big man, physically. With his glasses off and his attention on a man his youth was apparent, together with a certain handsomeness. His jaw was square and there was a hint of strength in the line of his body. Lewellyn thought again as he had before that this man must have been a harsh disappointment to Sharon. His appearance was more deceptive than most. There was irony in the fact that Sharon with her passion for truth and directness was married to the publisher of a paper which avoided issues as consistently as the *Courier* did.

Devore went a step beyond Sharon. Not only was he determined to settle a quarrel with words. He was unwilling to recognize the existence of a quarrel in the first place.

Devore put his glasses on his table and backed up to it so that he could grip the edges of it with his hands behind him.

"I've been wanting to talk to you, Lewellyn," he said slowly. "I've been waiting for a chance when we could have our talk alone. I have been a long time finding out, but I know all about you. All about you."

Steve frowned curiously. Suddenly he understood, and he was a little surprised.

"About La Mesa? Sharon didn't tell you about me in the beginning?"

"There was a great many things Sharon didn't see fit to tell me about, Lewellyn," Devore said with a sudden surge of bitterness. "I've had to find them out for myself. And I haven't liked them. You, least of all."

"Why?" Lewellyn countered. "The moon shines in Texas the same as it does in Abilene."

Devore's color darkened. Steve saw the man was stung. After a moment Devore shrugged.

"I had forgotten Texas. I'm not talking about La Mesa now, Lewellyn. I'm talking about Brokenbow. You were here when we came. I've often wondered if you knew Sharon would persuade me to move the *Courier* here. Why do you show up so often in town when your business is out on your land? Why is it you always manage to pass this office when you come in, even before you turn into the Grant for a drink? Is it Sharon, Lewellyn? Is it still Sharon?"

Devore's voice was a little unsteady. Lewellyn studied him carefully, impressed by a side of the man's nature which he had never before seen. Devore had a gall which could be touched, after all. And even a mild man could be unreasonably dangerous when a raw nerve was touched. Steve abandoned one speculation concerning Sharon to which he had occasionally devoted much time since she had arrived in Brokenbow. John Devore was in love with his wife. Almost grimly so. Lewellyn smiled and eased the moment.

"My business in town, John?" he repeated. "Sometimes it's one thing. Sometimes it's another. Today it was with Hal Fenton."

Devore kept his eyes steady, disbelief in them.

"So you step in here and the first thing you ask about is my wife!"

Impatience rose in Steve. He didn't want a quarrel. He had already walked through one since sunset. And in Brokenbow he was opposed to quarreling.

"All right, John," he said. "Suppose you give me a price on a little space in your paper, then."

"I'm not finished, Lewellyn!" the printer snapped. "I've been waiting to tell you this. Sharon wants no part of you. That's why she didn't tell me you'd worked for the old man. It was dead. She wanted it forgotten. Ugly stories about you have come up the trails from Texas.

I've heard some of them. You've got no place in Brokenbow. Sharon doesn't want you here. Her heart's wrapped up in this town. She wants it to be a fit place to live. Red whisky and hard men and quick guns won't make it so. She wants churches and schools and farmers, the kind that stick to their land. You let Sharon be, Lewellyn. You let the rest of us be. Strap on your gun. Get on your horse. Get out of Brokenbow!"

Devore checked himself. He was breathing strongly. His face was without color. Steve realized the man had gone farther than he had intended. It was not Devore's nature to lay down an ultimatum. The man pressed back against the table behind him, an uneasiness in his eyes too cringing to be a fear. Lewellyn knew he could break Devore in this instant. A hostile move, a flaring of his own anger, and the printer would retreat completely. For an instant Steve was tempted. Not out of antagonism toward Devore. He felt a grudging sympathy for the man. Fear, he thought, was a topheavy burden in Brokenbow. And it would grow heavier.

The temptation was because of Sharon. She had once boasted that when she married a man it would be one who strengthened her, who removed the limitations put on her by her womanhood. She had boasted she would marry a fighter who would fight in her own fashion. And there would be a satisfaction of sorts in stripping the tin of his armor from Devore for this reason. But Steve let it go.

"You read my mind, John," he said quietly. "I came in here to put a notice in your paper. I've got title to my homestead now. And I agree with you. I think my time has run out in Brokenbow. I want to run a notice my land is for sale."

Devore stared at Steve, his mind working openly behind his eyes in an attempt to discover the flaw in this — to rationalize what his ears had just heard. In this moment of silence Sharon stepped through the parted curtains leading to the quarters behind the office. There was no way to know how long she had been standing in the darkened doorway. Through most of his conversation with her husband, Steve thought. She came across the office, passing Devore, and leaned against the counter opposite Steve. More mature, more somber of face, but fuller of body, taller with pride, more beautiful than she had been in the *llanos*. More beautiful than she had been in the pool below the ford on Willow Creek. More beautiful and equally as sure. She pulled a pencil and a pad of copy paper from a shelf under the counter and squared them before her. She looked up. She met Steve's eyes.

"I used to wonder about this, Steve," she said. "This is the first time you've been in the office since we opened it. And you come now on business."

Steve was puzzled. Sharon's tone, her manner, suggested that they were alone, free to talk as either of them might wish. She seemed unaware of Devore behind her. And the puzzlement made

Steve uncomfortable.

"I want to run a notice," he said. "I want to sell my place."

"It's six dollars a column inch."

"An inch will be enough. You write it. Anybody interested can see Charlie Bissel. He'll handle it for me."

Sharon bent over the pad, writing swiftly with her pencil held in slightly ink-stained fingers. Lewellyn watched. The ink stains impressed him. He had not before thought that a newspaper could be a poor living. He had not thought of Sharon at all in terms of income, of money. He realized now that the ink was the same as the calluses on a ranch woman's hands. The *Courier* was no better a provider than ten sections of Texas greasewood. Sharon had gained little in three years. An old bitterness over the division between them rose. He checked it. Sharon looked up from the brief notice she had written. Her eyes probed his without friendliness.

"Running away, Steve?" she asked. Steve weighed this, then nodded slowly.

"Yes. Yes, I guess so. I tangled tonight with Hal Fenton. Words, but there's more in the book that'll have to come out. And Doc McKenna wants me with him — with some of the others. Which means more in the book. What I came to Brokenbow to find is gone. It's time for me to move."

"You won't, Steve —" Sharon said.

Devore pushed away from his table. He came

down to the counter at his wife's elbow.

"He said he would." Devore cut in raggedly. "Isn't that enough? I told him he'd better."

Sharon did not turn her body. Only her head. She turned it and looked blankly at her husband.

"Next time, try telling the wind to die when it's knocking the shutters down, John. You won't sound like any bigger a fool!"

Acid, almost savage. Contemptuous words which silenced Devore and turned his cheeks white. Sharon turned her eyes back to Lewellyn's face.

"I've had a long time to think about you, Steve. Maybe even to understand you. You won't leave Brokenbow. Not while the drovers are still here and men like Doctor McKenna reckless enough to come asking for you. Pete drank himself to death in Abilene after we moved there. Doctors told him whisky was killing him. They told him he'd die. He believed them. Whisky made him sick the last few months. Inside, he didn't want it. I think he even hated it. But he kept on drinking. You won't leave."

"You want it that way? You want me to stay?"

"You know how I wanted it. I know better now. A man doesn't change. He crawls on his knees or he beats others down. There doesn't seem to be any middle ground, where a man can roll up his sleeves and still stay inside the law. At least I haven't found it, Steve. And I've used up all of my chances."

Sharon pressed the point of her pencil against the top of the counter until the lead in it snapped with a small, sharp sound. Lewellyn shifted his weight and his boot rasped loudly on the floor. Devore put his hand on his wife's shoulder.

"By God, Sharon," he said quickly, "I'm not on my knees to anybody but you!"

"You couldn't have got the calluses you've got there in three years! That'll be six dollars, Steve. . . ."

Lewellyn reached for change. Devore dropped his hand from Sharon's shoulder. He backed a little away from her. Steve started for the door.

"You listen to this too, Lewellyn!" Devore said swiftly. He continued backing from his wife until he was again against his composing table. "You said you'd used up all your chances, Sharon. You remember that. Don't ever think you've turned up another one. Don't either one of you ever think you've turned up another one!"

Sharon turned. She put Steve's notice down on the table beside Devore. She indicated the framed type of a page on the rack.

"You haven't locked up yet, John. This can go in place of a filler cut. Supper's on when you've washed up."

Chapter 4

On the walk outside the *Courier* Steve was hailed. A man came along under the awning of the walk. Steve recognized his quick, bantam steps. They met in front of the building beside the *Courier*. The man was Jed Barnage. A frown was puckered up between his shrewd little eyes. He glanced at the newspaper office. Sharon or Devore moved in front of the lamp and cast a long shadow through the windows onto the street.

"Zoe was kind of looking for you up to the house tonight. The Missus too," Jed said. Steve nodded.

"Zoe told me."

"I was kind of looking for you too, Steve," Barnage went on. "It's getting to a place where we've either got to cut our hay in this town or leave it rot in the field. I figured you might have some ideas."

"— Since I'm a farmer?" Steve asked.

"Farmer, hell!" Barnage snorted. "What difference does it make what a man is? It's the way he thinks that counts."

Steve nodded.

"You're entitled to know, Jed," he said carefully. "I just gave Devore a notice to run on my section. I'm clearing out."

The frown deepened between Barnage's eyes.

"Maybe Bissel talked out of turn, Steve," he said. "On the other hand, you said I was entitled to know. And there's Zoe. She and the hardware store are all Ruth and me have got to show for a hell of a lot of living. Charlie told me you'd known Mrs. Devore in Texas. You clearing out on account of her?"

Steve shook his head.

"No. I did that once, Jed. A man doesn't travel the same trail very often. I'm getting out of Brokenbow because of the way I think. There's a tangle coming here with Fenton and his outfit. My way of handling a snarled line won't work here. Not when it's you and McKenna and the like against Fenton and Sam Dreen and some of the others who ride for Willow Creek. You can make laws, and you've got Keown to make them stick. You'll do best that way. A man without a gun doesn't get shot."

Jed scuffed his boot on the walk. He looked up suddenly.

"You sound like Devore's wife!"

"I'm trying to, Jed," Steve answered quietly.

Barnage swore. A soft sound, without sulphur. He continued to look at Steve.

"If I didn't know you better, I'd make another guess," he said slowly. "I'd figure you'd heard that Hal Fenton has sobered up a little since the game tonight in the Spur, and is claiming he'll run Sock McKenna and you both out of town before he's through. That ain't it, of course. So you must have heard about Westfall."

Steve looked his question.

"I'm looking for Keown," Barnage went on. "Maybe he's heard too, and don't want any part of it. Can't find him anyways. Westfall was in town today. He pulled out about sunset. When he got home he found his place at Tie Creek burned to the ground. Grass fire had come down over the hill. Took his barn first. Then the house. When it got to the creek, it died."

"Lightning?" Steve suggested with a full knowledge of the inadequacy of the explanation.

"Sure, lightning," Barnage agreed bitterly. "Kansas lightning. Damned dangerous stuff, Steve! First, it sent a couple of strangers around to Westfall three weeks ago with an offer of a dollar an acre for his place. Next, it left a letter at the postoffice with a pretty scary warning about him getting off Tie Creek. Then it waited till today, when him and the whole family was in town. It opened his barn and corral and turned loose all his stock. Then it hit the grass over the hill, where it wouldn't burn more than enough graze to wipe him out before the creek killed it. Westfall don't like that kind of lightning. Neither do I!"

"Where's Westfall now?" Lewellyn asked quietly.

"The family's at my house. Ruth is looking to them. I think Jim's at the Grant. He's shook up plenty. Look, Steve, circle with me. Keown's got to be some place. We better get him. There might be trouble. Fenton and some of his crew are still in town."

"Go ahead. You find Ord, if you've got to have him. I'll be at the Grant, Jed."

Relief crossed Barnage's face. The shrewdness which made him a good trader surfaced in his eyes for a moment.

"I thought you said you were selling out of this, Steve," he said.

Lewellyn shrugged.

"You get Keown," he repeated.

Barnage stepped around him and moved on up the walk, the worn heels of his boots beating a quick, light rhythm on the walk. Steve stepped down into the dust of the street and angled across toward the Grant. He wasn't sure that Barnage would accomplish much in finding the marshal of Brokenbow. This was the season he assigned for his own destination at Bissel's saloon.

Ord Keown and himself, he believed, were in many ways cut from similar patterns. The conditioning of their lives had made them hard. Both understood a bluff and its uses. Both possessed the ability to probe deeply enough to reach hidden softness in others. And neither of them were hampered by the accumulation of borrowed ethics and principles which generally cluttered a man's judgment and decision and even his emotions. Principle was fundamental and simple. As fundamental and simple as the straight blade of a knife. One side was thin, honed to a fine feather-cutting edge. The other was broad, blunt, for stiffening and strength.

Killers, Steve supposed, if the ability to kill swiftly, decisively, and without compunction when judgment demanded, made a killer. Gunmen, if patient physical conditioning and necessity and swift reflexive skill with a gun made a gunman. A dangerous kind. Respected, but never fully trusted. Always a little apart from the full warmth of friendship which lay between other men.

But there was a difference between Keown and himself. Keown made a trade of his gun. He was an implement of the law and lived by it. His hardness and his dominance were trade skills. He used them meticulously as such. And protection of his reputation was a restraint on the marshal which Steve Lewellyn did not have, just as his badge was a justification Steve could not claim. Keown would walk lightly in order to hold his job. He would walk lightly always. To Steve this had always been compromise. A badge altered neither fundamental, right or wrong.

Reaching the false front of the Grant, Lewellyn turned. Barnage was far up the street, near the livery, toward which he was obviously heading. Across the street a movement caught Steve's attention. A man had issued from the narrow passage which ran back alongside the *Courier* building. The only street access, except through the office itself, to the living quarters behind the newspaper. Devore was still in the office. Sharon was not. The man from the passageway glanced both ways along the street, then swung off in the direction already taken by Jed Barnage. Steve recognized Ord Keown. He was mildly puzzled by the marshal's business behind the *Courier*, but he shrugged it off. He was tempted for a moment to hail, then let this go also.

Jim Westfall was bitter and he might be drunk. He needed a little counsel and some hard thinking to set him right on his feet again — to cool him down. Another man from the homesteads might be able to do this better than Keown. If not, Jed would meet Ord at the upper end of the street and bring him back, anyway. Lewellyn pushed against the doors of the Grant and stepped into Bissel's saloon.

His entrance made little stir. Three Willow Creek riders, apparently liking Bissel's whisky better than that available at the Spur, were bellied-up to the forward section of the bar. Jim Westfall was a little beyond them, staring moodily at a bottle in front of him. Its level had already been lowered considerably. The man was drunk, the hurt in him wrapped in whisky but in no way eased. The Swedish homesteader who had been in the Spur earlier in the evening was at Westfall's elbow. Lewellyn moved past both of them and stopped in front of Charlie Bissel. Bissel reached down a bottle of Roanoke.

He glanced from Steve to the two groups on up the bar and made a wry face.

"Ever smoke a loaded cigar, Steve?" he asked softly. "One you knew was loaded?"

Lewellyn shook his head. Bissel nodded at Westfall and the Swede.

"That's what them two farmers are doing — and on purpose. Just chewing and waiting for the damned thing to go off in their faces! Drink up and get out of here."

"I just came in," Steve protested, and he tipped his glass. Charlie Bissel snorted.

"Want to see the smoke, eh? Steve, damn it, you can't ride two horses at once! Not and live long. Either you've got to take off your gloves or you got to ball up your fists and swing."

Lewellyn grinned. Bissel said something under his breath and moved down to another customer. Steve saw the two Willow Creek riders watching him with more than casual interest. He slid along the bar to the Swede's elbow. He spoke around him to Westfall.

"I heard about your place, Westfall," he said quietly. "Think I'd like to ride out there with you tomorrow. Maybe we could turn up something interesting. Your wife's up at Barnage's. Zoe's looking for me. Want to drift that way with me?"

Westfall looked long at Steve. Finally he lifted the glass in front of him, saw it was empty, and poured it full again. He drank this off in a pair of hard swallows. He made no answer. The Swede looked at Steve and frowned with an admixture

143

of apology and concern. The front door opened with a noisy, wide swing. Keown stood in its center, hands braced out to keep the slats from swinging back on him. Beyond Keown stood Barnage, the puckering of worry still between his eyes.

Keown made a slow, careful survey of the room. He spoke over his shoulder to Barnage.

"I try to keep my rounds regular at night, Jed," he said sharply. "It's quiet, here. I don't like being pulled in when there's no call!"

"You got to burn yourself on a fuse before you'll admit it's lighted, Ord?" Barnage snapped.

"Leave Westfall be," Keown said evenly. "He's a right to a drink if he needs it and I reckon he does. He's too smart to start something in my town. 'Way too smart —"

The exchange between Barnage and Keown was not loud, but Lewellyn, beside the Swede homesteader, heard it plainly. So did the two Willow Creek riders. It altered the expression on their faces. Not much. Just a little. But the Swede did not act as if he had heard. Neither did Westfall. And the whole thing seemed pointless to Lewellyn. What a man didn't hear he couldn't consider. Keown's conception of his duty was too narrow. So was the scope of the warning he had given Westfall.

The marshal turned in the doorway of the saloon and stepped back onto the walk. Jed Barnage shouldered angrily past him and came on in. The door swung closed. The two Willow Creek riders turned their attention again to their drinks. Barnage came on down and turned in at Steve's elbow. He had hardly breasted the bar when the front door swung again. A single man came in. He was small for a rider, set compactly into a hard, shortened frame. His eyes swept the room as thoroughly and nearly as swiftly as Keown's had. They touched Lewellyn, lingered briefly in recognition, and moved on to Westfall.

The farmer had glanced up at the movement of the doors, apprising Lewellyn he might have heard Keown's counsel and his warning, after all. Seeing the newcomer in the doorway, Westfall wheeled around and pressed his back against the bar. The Swede, between Lewellyn and Westfall, pivoted also. And with these two, the Willow Creek riders also turned, so that the four of them stood in a tight row, their faces all turned toward the newcomer. One of the riders spoke with ease of familiarity.

"Hello, Sam. Drink — ?"

Sam Dreen nodded curtly without taking his eyes from Westfall. The farmer's burned face was dark, his eyes hot. His fingers were white as they gripped the bar behind him.

"Will you still give me a dollar an acre for my place, Dreen?" he asked.

Dreen shot a second glance around the room. His eyes again met Steve's. They were challenging. Lewellyn kept his answering gaze bland. Barnage stepped around him and spoke across

145

the Swede to Westfall.

"Jennie's been asking for you, Jim," he said swiftly. "She's at my place. She wants you. It's been a hard day for her, too."

Westfall's head settled stubbornly on his neck. He continued to glare at Sam Dreen. Dreen spoke surly to him.

"Who the hell are you?"

Westfall pushed out from the bar. His voice came up on a ragged edge.

"I'm the dirt farmer you bull-dozed at Tie Creek," he said harshly. "I'm the farmer you and another Willow Creek rider I'd never seen before tried to buy some grassland from. I'm the farmer you burned out tonight!"

"Good God!" Jed Barnage muttered to Lewellyn. "Dreen must have been the one that made Jim that offer!"

"You're crazy, farmer!" Dreen answered Westfall insolently.

Steve spoke then. Quietly.

"Get out of here, Dreen. Now!"

He succeeded only in drawing the attention of one of the two Willow Creek riders. Jed Barnage backed and started toward Westfall. The farmer smiled crookedly.

"Crazy? Could be. But I'd rather be crazy than dead!" he said. He moved, with his body wound tight. Aggressive movement. Whether it was a reach for a gun under the skirt of his coat or a gesture with a clenched fist was not clear. And the fuse went.

146

Half way to Westfall, Barnage jerked his gun with the others. The two Willow Creek riders flung out a pair of yards from the bar, swung like a team, and fired at Westfall. He took both of their shots without moving in his tracks and lifted a gun from his coat. He fired once with this at Dreen. His shot went wide, scoring the surface of Bissel's bar. The Swede homesteader, a little behind Westfall and in the line of fire from Dreen, dropped to the floor, firing as he fell. One of the two Willow Creek riders barked with hurt. And at the end of this, Jed Barnage got his first shot away, slow and out of line.

Dreen fired twice. The first shot blinded the big Swede on the floor with splinters from the planking. The second spilled Jed Barnage flat. The untouched Willow Creek rider wheeled a quarter around and dropped the muzzle of his weapon almost into Jed's face. Lewellyn had stayed clear. He had not thought this would happen. He had thought he could check Dreen and he had thought Westfall would require more driving than this. So it was an error in judgment. An error in judgment to have come in off the street — to have gotten into this at all. But he was here and Jed Barnage was a friend. As much a friend as he had in Brokenbow. One to whom he owed a debt. And Jed had as little business in this as he did himself. He drew and emptied his gun without breaking the rhythm of its firing. When he hit empty chambers the Willow Creek hand who had been above Barnage was broken against the foot of the bar, the doors of the Grant were shattered, and Dreen and the earlier wounded Willow Creek man were gone.

The Swede homesteader stood up, dabbing at his eyes, flushing them out with their own water. Charlie Bissel shoved his head up from behind the bar. He glanced at the room, at the men down. He swung toward Lewellyn without either condemnation or praise.

"Christ! What'd you use, a scattergun? You've notched your tree now, Steve!"

Lewellyn bent over Barnage, doubled up on his knees, hooked his hands under Jed's arms, and lifted the hardware man up beside him.

"How is it, Jed?"

"Thigh," Barnage said. "Get me home."

The Swede moved close. Steve spoke over his shoulder to him.

"Get Doc McKenna. No, the back way, you fool. Willow Creek'll be running four feet deep down the street out front in a couple of minutes!"

"You know where Jed lives?" Charlie Bissel asked.

The Swede nodded, but paused a moment, looking at Jim Westfall. The farmer had backed again against the bar, but where he had been tight and erect, he was bent, now.

"You're hit, Jim!" Jed Barnage breathed. Pulling away from Lewellyn, he staggered a step to Westfall's side. Lewellyn crossed behind him, putting his shoulder up under one of the farmer's arms. Westfall rocked his head back and forth. The Swede wheeled and started on a run for the back door.

"I'll bring the Doc here!" he called.

"In the belly," Westfall said with effort. "Twice!"

Lewellyn stooped, reached under the man's knees, and lifted his long frame up onto the bar. Charlie Bissel poured a stiff drink and held it to the farmer's lips. But Westfall's mouth was closed. When it did open, a moment later, a light-breathed string of formless words gushed out, and his breathing stopped. Charlie Bissel looked at the drink he held, then tossed it off.

"You didn't plow a very long furrow, brother," he said quietly to the dead man, "but you sure as hell turned over the sod!"

"Send McKenna along to Jed's house when he gets here, Charlie," Lewellyn snapped. "I've got to get Jed out of here."

He lifted Barnage, turned the man so that he faced him, and sat him astraddle his hips, where he could hold him with one hand if there was need. Shoving his own gun into his belt, he hooked up Barnage's still partially loaded one and slid out the back door of the Grant into the darkness of the alley.

Chapter 5

Socrates McKenna came into the Barnage parlor with a shotgun under his arm. He stood this in the corner behind the door and slid out of his coat. Jed straightened apologetically on the settee.

"Howdy, Doc," he said.

McKenna growled and ran a square hand through the erect tangle of his thick red hair.

"Jed Barnage, you're a damned fool!" he said with conviction.

"You could be right, Doc," Jed agreed sheepishly. He eased back down. McKenna called for scissors, blandly explaining that he couldn't find his own when he threw his instruments into his case. Lewellyn glanced within the little bag. The scant supply of surgical steel within it would have been barely enough to satisfy a moderately finicky rancher who had some beef to castrate. McKenna seemed to feel they were ample, except for the missing scissors. These were brought.

Hot water was carried in. Even in Brokenbow women knew that blood meant a need for scalding water and it was already on the stove in the kitchen. Ruth Barnage carried down a thick, spotless sheet from a chest in the upstairs hall.

150

McKenna arranged these things carelessly around him. He wormed Jed out of his pants, but left them dangling confiningly around the wounded man's ankles. He opened the back flap of Jed's underdrawers and with a nice concern for the heavy woolens, pulled the opening thus available around over Jed's thigh, avoiding cutting the material. He studied the dark, welling wound for a moment, then straightened.

"Get out!" he said. "All of you get out. Jed is going to raise hell. If he don't, I will."

Lewellyn moved out with Ruth Barnage. Zoe came behind them and closed the door into the parlor. Westfall's wife stopped Ruth and Lewellyn in the hallway. Zoe moved on past. Jennie Westfall was large, plump, and shabbily dressed. But there was considerable youth in her color and in her firm cheeks. Strain had dragged a tight line across her full lips, but she eased it enough to be gentle with Ruth.

"How is he?" she asked.

Ruth passed a reddened hand across her eyes and shook her head.

"He'll be all right," Lewellyn said quietly.

Upstairs one of the Westfall youngsters began to wail. Outraged protest against strange surroundings and events beyond childhood understanding. Jennie Westfall murmured an apology and climbed the stairs. Ruth moved away from Steve, going on into her kitchen. He opened a side door in the hall and stepped out onto the long porch on the north side of the house. Zoe was standing by the railing just outside the drawn shades of the room in which Sock McKenna had already begun his painful work. Steve crossed to her and touched her shoulder. He meant the gesture to be one of commiseration. However, the neckline of Zoe's dress had slipped a little to one side and the contact was of flesh against flesh and more electric than Steve had anticipated. Zoe turned swiftly and the turn pressed her body lightly against him. Steve's fingers slid along under her ear. Her head tipped back a little. Inside the room behind them Jed Barnage bit down sulphurously on a moan. Zoe flinched and her head lowered. Steve gripped her shoulder again, suddenly very aware of the softness and the firmness under his touch. He slanted his head at the moon climbing above the town.

"Doc would make a man sweat while he was dressing a hangnail," he said. "Jed's all right. You said I needed that moon. Maybe I do. And so do you. Come on. We'll talk."

Zoe glanced at the curtained windows, then gave way, walking beside him. They went down the steps and around the rear corner of the house to a kind of arbor under some chicken wire and stringy cucumber vines. There was a long, wide bench under this and a table in one corner where Ruth occasionally served supper on hot nights. Zoe sat down on the bench, waited for Steve's arm to slide behind her, and leaned back against it. A shaft of moonlight angled through the vines, highlighting the softness of her parted lips, the roundness of her chin, and the long lines of her throat sweeping down to the curve of shoulder and breast. She lifted Steve's free hand, clasped it between her own, and held it on her lap. Unstudied, possessive, and — Steve supposed — skilful enough.

Zoe's beauty was freshness and substance, an unashamed and thinly veiled ardor. There was goodness, if not fineness, in her. And spirit enough for any man. She was not as Steve remembered Sharon Lynch. But she was challenge. He felt it. His fingers slid under her arm and tightened against her body. She turned her head and smiled lazily at him for a moment. And then, as though she had forgotten something more important — or as a provocation — she stiffened a little and frowned.

"Doc was right, Steve," she said. "Dad is a fool!"

In this moment Lewellyn didn't give a damn for Jed Barnage and less for talking about him. His mind had eased, gone vacant. The moon was in his eyes. His senses were absorbed. But he had a feeling of inadequacy with women. They understood flesh and could make a game of it, which he could not. He forced attention to what Zoe said.

"Why?" he asked raggedly.

"Dad's a hardware man. All he knows about guns is the kind of boxes they come in. He didn't have to mix in Jim Westfall's trouble. You and

153

Alex Christofferson and the rest of the home-steaders would have kept on buying wire and staples from him if he'd have stayed here in the house after supper tonight instead of going back up town. And what did he get for trying to help Jim. A bullet in the leg and loss of the business he's been doing with the Willow Creek crews. Maybe that's only a beginning. Westfall lost. He was bound to lose. Dad didn't help. He couldn't. Neither did you, Steve. Jim's dead. Dad should have thought of mother. He should have thought of me. There may be worse trouble coming because of this — and we could have been out of it, all of us!"

"It's your town, Zoe, same as it's Jed's," Steve said. "You can't get out of that. And maybe Jed was thinking of you. Maybe he didn't want to crawl on his knees in his own town. Maybe he didn't want you and your mother crawling on your knees too."

A feeling of repetition and of helplessness swept Lewellyn. This was a long way from Texas. But the problems were the same, and women were the same. Zoe's argument and his own sounded in his mind like the echo of the long talk he had had with Sharon by stove-light in the bunk shack on Willow Creek. And the night was the same. There was silence and softness and warmth and his struggle was again for a balance between conviction and desire.

"You sound just like dad!" Zoe said petulantly. "Hal Fenton doesn't care whether we

154

crawl, wriggle, or fly in Brokenbow! He wants some grass for his cattle —" Zoe paused. She leaned back against Steve's shoulder. She tilted her face up. She raised his hand from her lap and pulled it against her diaphragm. "Is a little grass so important, Steve — ?" she breathed.

Lewellyn forced an answer, swiftly, defensively.

"Until there's a railroad down into the Texas cattle country itself, Fenton and the others will be driving north for shipment. First to Dodge and Abilene, now to Brokenbow, later to some town further west. Fenton is driving four hundred miles. Four hundred miles burns up a lot of fat. He's got to have grass at the end of the drive to get back that weight. And when there's somebody already on that grass, there's bound to be trouble —"

He stopped. Zoe was still looking up at him. She twisted a little, nestling closer. She smiled. The twisting made the starched front of her dress stand out from her neck line. The moon was higher than Steve's eyes and as penetrating. Its light made a magic of her breasts. Steve's throat constricted, choking off the words in it. He freed his hand and pulled Zoe to him. Roughly. She laughed with a tantalizing softness.

"You have such a hard time being a farmer, Steve," she murmured under his ear. "And it's so easy . . . if you have the right kind of help. A plow and a little white house and a fence. It's as

155

big as the world and you can stay inside the fence . . . if you've got something to keep you there. Something you want. Something you want more than trouble. Something you want more than anything. . . ."

Steve found her lips and silenced them. They blossomed like an opening flower under his own. Zoe's arms went around his neck, fiercely and with abandon. Lewellyn had an illusion of catapulting through space, rushing in the company of a roaring wind toward something. When the wind was crescendo, Zoe drew a little away. She was still smiling. Confidence was bright in her eyes.

"You wouldn't be too hard to change, Steve," she said softly.

Lewellyn shook his head stubbornly.

"I tried once. I tried hard, Zoe."

"But not with me. . . ." she murmured.

Steve bent his head again. Once more the wind roared in his ears. In his mind a thought stirred. This was a woman, bidding for peace as Sharon had once bid. This was Jed Barnage's daughter, trading for a husband and a way of life. But the thought could get no further in his consciousness than the first phrase. This was a woman — and he had been lonely in Brokenbow.

Pride writhed a little in Lewellyn. To be the aggressor with a woman had seemed important to him. What he had known with Sharon he had long thought he would not share with another —

even after Sharon's marriage and her sharing with John Devore. And Jed Barnage was his friend. These things and the dustiness of the arbor, the too-full light of the moon, the knowledge that privacy here was an illusion. But here was escape from bitterness which Charlie Bissel's best whisky did not afford. Here was surcease which the hardest labor he had put in on his homestead could not achieve. And here, also, might be truth.

His rush through space had become meteoric. He closed his eyes to the shadows in the arbor, to dust and dishevelment and the house behind them.

Doc McKenna's harsh voice was like a screen of sand flung against his face on a sudden gust of wind.

"Your pa wants a drink of whisky, Zoe. You know where the bottle is?"

Zoe straightened unhurriedly. She raised her hand to her hair and smoothed it. McKenna, uncompromising in this as in anything, stood in the arch of the arbor doorway without embarrassment or apology. Zoe stood up and smoothed her skirt.

"I'll get it for him," she told McKenna.

"Save me some," the doctor warned sharply. "And maybe Steve could do with a shot."

"Why, Doc, you mean that personally?" she asked in mock protest. She grinned at a slight change in McKenna's ruddy color and bent close to Steve, so that her lips were at his ear for a moment. "The grass, Steve — remember?" she breathed. "Is it so important — now?"

She turned then, her dress flaring so that it brushed both McKenna's knees and the framing of the doorway as she passed him, and she ran back up the walk toward the house. McKenna came on slowly into the arbor and dropped down onto the wide seat, where the boards were still warm with the heat of Zoe's body.

"I'm sorry, Lewellyn —" he said quietly.

Steve supposed he should feel resentment. He did not. He shook his head slightly.

"Forget it, McKenna. I'm glad you didn't wait any longer."

"So am I," McKenna agreed slowly. "You've got some thinking to do, Lewellyn. You've got to figure where you fit in this town. You've got to know where you belong and how you feel — about a lot of things. And in a hurry, I think."

"Maybe, if I was staying, McKenna. But I'm not. I put a notice in the paper tonight. I'm selling out. I'm drifting."

Lewellyn thought McKenna would ask the same question Sharon had. He thought the doctor would want to know if he was running away. Maybe from something he couldn't face. McKenna's brows went up sharply with interest. But he asked a different question.

"Before you kill Hal Fenton?"

Steve was startled. McKenna was a fundamentalist. He knew where to dig for roots. Lewellyn shook his head.

"So I won't have to," he said.

McKenna smiled.

"You won't make it, Lewellyn," he said knowingly. "A man doesn't change like that. A woman can't change him like that. Ten women can't. What he wants and what he thinks can't change him. There's a fence right down the middle of his vest. One side is right. The other's wrong. And the fence is there to stay. He was born with it. He'll die with it — or because of it. You're fighting yourself. Pitch in with the town, Lewellyn. Fight Fenton — with the rest of us. It'll make you feel better."

Steve shook his head again. His mouth set with finality. McKenna rose and shrugged.

"All right. But you're not going to walk the street very comfortable until you've got your place sold and you're ready to ride, unless some of the rest of us sort of stand behind you a little. They tell me that was Fenton's nephew you cut in two at the Grant tonight. Hal and his drovers love you next to me — and there seems to be some sort of a Texas score added to it. I've got to get up and stitch a crease in Sam Dreen's arm. You stick to the hotel tonight and get around to see me early in the morning. You saved Jed's life tonight. Maybe Zoe's paid you off for that. If she hasn't, the rest of us will. We'd admire to have you stay. If you won't, we'll see you're covered till you're gone."

McKenna's advice was without steam. It was practical. So was his offer of friendliness. Steve accepted them as such.

"Thanks, McKenna. I'll see you in the morning, then."

Doc moved off up the walk. Lewellyn groped, found his hat under the bench, dusted it, and set it on his head. Avoiding the lights of the house, he struck off across lots toward the bulk of Whisky Row and the hotel.

Chapter 6

Barnage had a team and a dray which he used to ferry freight from the station on the south side of town to his store and for occasional deliveries into the country when a customer was in need of such service. He kept the team in a makeshift stable at the back of his lot, a couple of hundred feet from the house. A wagon track of sorts ran from this stable along behind the buildings on the north side of the main street and parallel with it. At Kinner's hotel, which was set back farther than the other buildings, this track turned and swung out to the walk. It made a suitable path back to the hotel.

Lewellyn walked slowly, without hurry, ordering his mind. The moon, which had early been bright, had thinned. Cloud had fuzzed in across the crown of the ridge, filtering out early radiance. The night had darkened, so that the back lots along Lewellyn's course were all silence and shadow. The street — the town — seemed remote. Inward turning of thought was automatic in the darkness and silence. Thought became conclusion; conclusion became purpose. Space was again something man traversed afoot or in a saddle laboriously. The wind was gone from his ears. Lewellyn could see Zoe

Barnage plainly.

She was more than a promise. She was fulfillment. She was honest. But she was a woman, with few complexities beyond a woman's way of thinking. Beyond an eternal trading and compromise against struggle. Robbed of independence of action and belief and even thought by the dependence of her kind. Dependence upon a man. Dependence on the law. Dependence upon one kind of god or another, and with but one confidence — her body and its power over a man.

A home could be built on this, Steve supposed. A life. Many had been. But the foundation was too narrow. Zoe would hang his gun on a peg on the wall. She would bend his back to a plow, his thinking to the security of their own possessions. And she would take him to bed. It wasn't enough. Dangerously close. Generously offered. But not enough.

Zoe's breath was momentarily against Lewellyn's cheek again in the darkness. His hands clenched. He had two reasons, now, to get out of Brokenbow. Neither was a compromise. He had made himself a farmer. When the pressure of violence grew too strong, a farmer took what profit he could and moved on to a new beginning. This had been Sharon's preachment. He was keeping faith with it. He was protecting his own interests. Only his own. And he did not want Zoe Barnage. Only a part of her, and that part too much. It was time to move on.

162

Thought of Sharon, inadvertent and abstract, became something suddenly material. What Doc McKenna's appearance under the arbor had shattered returned now with a somehow multiplied intensity. Explosiveness was in Steve. Physical restraint which hurt. Sharon was in his mind, not Zoe. Sharon's body was white in the moonlight. Sharon's voice was in his ear. Her warmth was against his thigh and his shoulder, her heart hammering softly under his hand.

Lewellyn halted with a soft oath at his edginess, at Zoe, at McKenna. He fumbled in his pocket for tobacco and papers and rolled a cigarette with an unsteadiness which further shook him. As he reached for a match, the sound of a voice drew his attention. He looked about him. He was behind Barnage's store. The hotel was yet rods away. Rank weeds grew waist high on both sides of the alley — like wagon track. Back of the store, across the wagon track and fifty feet into the weeds, there was an old top-buggy with a broken wheel, the hubless shaft of the axle supported on an up-ended box. Lewellyn glanced at this curiously, but the voice came again, a woman's voice, soft and much closer at hand. He turned his head.

Old grass and weeds had been cleared from a little patch of ground beside the rear corner of Barnage's store. Steve thought Jed had piled some lumber there the fall before. The pile was gone now, and a spring wild growth had come up, soft and short and velvety. The voice was there. The woman was there. Sitting in the darkness with her feet out before her on the softness of the grass and her back against the wall of Jed's store, a man's head cradled across her lap and breast. Thirty feet away, unnoticed, with a match already pressed against his nail for lighting, Steve recognized the black sheen and cut of Ord Keown's box-tailed coat.

Keown shifted a little. The woman's voice came again. The eternal invitation of protest. The two figures locked in the long, straining silence of an embrace. The match in Lewellyn's fingers snapped in two. He reached slowly into his pocket for another, set it against his nail, and flicked it alight. He raised the flame to the too-wet, unwanted cigarette between his lips, drawing twice with unnecessary care. When he snapped the match to the ground and out, Sharon Devore and Keown were on their feet. Steve moved toward them, thinking wryly that the shoe was now on another foot. Ord Keown's face had the white, set, defensive look which he knew must have been on his own when Sock McKenna walked into the arbor behind Jed Barnage's house.

" 'Evening, Sharon — Ord —" he said quietly. His quietness stung. He meant it to do so.

"Lewellyn!" Keown spat the name from his lips. A little shard broken from the thin and whetted edge of his temper, his tautness. Steve swung his eyes from the place where Sharon and Ord had been sitting to embrace the rankness and the litter of this back lot. Keown moved slowly, intently forward. Lewellyn could see the man's torture. His own integrity, roasting over the ebbing flames within him. The law of Brokenbow, on its knees in the weeds. Steve used Sock McKenna's words, under the arbor.

"I'm sorry, Ord —"

"You Indian-footed son of a bitch!" Keown said tonelessly and almost soundlessly. He was a yard from Lewellyn. An intense, white-faced silhouette against the dark shadow of Barnage's store. Lewellyn felt the bite of his white anger, the impact of his intensity, and he understood Keown's lethal strength, his ability to retain unruffled balance in the tumbled, changing, thankless channel of the law. Physical perceptions sharpened. This was beyond words. And Lewellyn had only emptiness with which to meet it.

Beyond Ord's shoulder he saw Sharon. The Sharon who had been in his mind. The woman who had taken all that Zoe Barnage so honestly offered and used it for her own. The woman he had built out of recollections and dreaming, her body still aglow with another's caresses, stolen, clandestine, and therefore ugly. A man wanted a table with a scoured top or a washed cloth for eating. He wanted clean grass or the fresh linen of a bed for love. A woman should want as much. Lewellyn remembered only to keep his hands high, away from his gun. This should not go that far, and only he could prevent it.

Keown struck with the physical economy of a diamondback and with nearly the same incredible swiftness. The blow cleared Lewellyn's defense and exploded somewhere along the line of his jaw. The night flared brilliantly and tipped crazily. Dry weed growth snapped under him as he went down. Keown came in. Lewellyn crouched on his heels and came up slowly, his eyes on Keown's boots. But Sharon had leaped across. She was clinging to Ord's arm. Clinging there like a woman from the back room of a saloon with a drunk on her hands.

"Ord, no! No! Please, God, Ord, no! It's all right —" Keown's head turned slowly. He looked full in her face for a moment. He bent and lifted his hat, which he had shaken loose with the violence of his sudden strike. Lewellyn straightened.

"You're a damned fool, Ord!" he said levelly. "There was no call for that."

He turned. Sharon released the marshal and caught Lewellyn's arm.

"Steve, wait! I've got to talk to you. Ord, let me handle this. Please go. Let me talk to Steve."

Keown glanced briefly at Lewellyn, then turned on his heel and struck off through the weeds alongside the building toward the walk in front of Barnage's store.

Lewellyn disengaged his arm from Sharon's grip. The taste of blood was in the corner of his mouth. He found his kerchief and wiped at it.

"You're afraid I'm going to talk?" he suggested.

"Would I be afraid of talk, Steve?" she asked softly. "No. I'm afraid, all right. But not of talk. I'm afraid you don't understand."

Steve smiled tightly.

"Understand?" he said. "I should understand better than anyone. I know what you can do to a night and a man. I remember. I know what Ord's carrying away inside of him, right now."

"Not Ord," Sharon said patiently. "Me. You've got to understand, Steve. Me, John — the whole thing."

Steve nodded.

"All right," he agreed drily. "I'll try."

"I made a mistake with John," Sharon said swiftly.

"A newspaper seemed the right kind of a weapon. And John — his bigness, his quietness, his unhurried thinking. He couldn't be baited, Steve. I knew that. He wouldn't use his hands for fists — only for setting type. And he didn't own a gun. I came from the *llanos*, Steve. I had never met a coward until I met John Devore. How could I know?"

"All right," Steve said. "He cheated you. The tin came off when you got him home. You have to have steel. I know that. So you cheat him in return. Does it make any difference? Does that make his paper honest?"

"No. But there are things more important than the paper, Steve. Hal Fenton is going to

167

force trouble on Brokenbow. Soon. And Brokenbow is my town. I came here to have my start. Brokenbow is all I have to defend. And the law is its only defense. Ord is lonely. No man can stand alone. If I can give him strength, if I can stand behind him until Fenton has his grass and the homesteaders are quiet again, if there is no violence and a peaceful settlement of claims and quarrels — if I do these things, haven't I made up for my mistake in Abilene?"

"If you could do that, you'd be the left hand of God," Lewellyn said bluntly. "But you're not. Neither is Ord Keown. You're a woman, Sharon. Ord's a man — maybe your kind of man. But it doesn't go past that. It's so damned simple. Keep it that way."

Sharon caught her breath and pulled her full lower lip in under her teeth. Lewellyn thought she was going to cry — or swear. He didn't know which.

"Here —"

He reached out for her, pulled her tightly against him. He bent his head, used force to tip her face upward, and ground his lips against hers. Without tenderness. With elemental purpose. One of Sharon's hands raked the side of his face. She twisted deftly and one knee drove against him savagely. She had learned much. Steve wondered if Devore had taught her this defensiveness. The thought further darkened his dislike for the printer. He continued to hold her, using his strength freely, until she quieted. This

168

had been his purpose. But its accomplishment did not give him freedom.

He was clamped in a vise. Sharon was also caught between its jaws, so that a compulsion beyond the strength of either locked them together. This was the arbor under the cucumber vines. This was Sharon's protest at Ord Keown's caress. And it was more than either. It was savage, engulfing. It was lightning — shot thunder and the roar of a flood. With an effort which tore like the tearing of flesh, Lewellyn released the woman in his arms and stepped back.

"You see?" he said roughly. "I understand. I've been hungry, too!"

He wheeled and walked unsteadily, swiftly, along the wagon track toward Kinner's hotel.

Chapter 7

Lewellyn climbed the exterior rear stairs to the
second floor of Kinner's hotel. He felt like a man
who had three times poured himself full of
whisky beyond his limit, sobering between each
bout, so that now physical exhaustion hung
heavily on him, his mouth was foul, his head
hammered, and he was as flat-bellied as though
nausea had emptied him completely. He braced
the door of his room with a chair and went to bed
without lighting his light.

The night hung oppressively about him, sti-
fling even thought. He slept fitfully, but without
satisfaction, troubled by fragments of perception
from the evening which returned to torment his
body with recollection. He rose early in the
morning, but waited, dressed, in his room until
after eight.

He was brushing his hair, certain he had
waited long enough for the town to be fully astir
and almost ready to descend to the street, when
a hand rattled the knob of his door. Remembering McKenna's warning that Willow Creek
would make his presence in town at least difficult since the affair in the Grant last night, he
scooped up his gun, kicked the chair-back from
under the knob of the door, sprung the latch and

jerked the door open. Kinner stood outside, a stupid look on his fat face and the fresh smell of morning whisky on his breath.

Kinner had one key on his big ring in his hand and the folds of a stack of reasonably clean linen over his arm. He blinked and ran a loose tongue over his lips.

"I — uh — the wrong room —" he stuttered uneasily. Then he caught hold of himself. "No. No, I thought you didn't come back last night. I thought you had gone —"

"Why?" Lewellyn snapped. "I rented the room."

Kinner colored and started backing down the hall.

"No reason," he said placatingly. "No reason —"

Lewellyn let him go. He turned back into the room for his hat and belt. He thought he understood. Kinner had soft pads on his feet. He went everywhere. His ears were as big as his capacity for whisky. There was talk this morning in the bars about him. Kinner had heard something there. That Steve Lewellyn was quitting town, certainly. Maybe on his own initiative. Maybe because he had to. Steve was a little curious as to which way Kinner had heard it. But he realized it made little difference. He shrugged and took the main stairs to the lower floor.

There was no one in the lobby. He stopped for a moment on the veranda to let the sunlight narrow his eyes. The street was quiet, clear save for a few men about early business toward the upper end, near the livery. He stepped onto the walk. As he passed the *Courier* office, he glanced at it, but the center shade on the front door was drawn and there was nothing else to see. The living quarters at the rear had no windows on the street. He turned into Kei Lin's restaurant, a few doors farther on.

The place was empty, save for the Swedish farmer who had gone after Doc McKenna from the Grant the night before. He looked up, dusted his hands, and grinned in obvious reference to the tangle in front of Charlie Bissel's bar.

"Makes a man hungry," he said.

Lewellyn sat down without comment. Kei Lin came out of his kitchen cubicle and waddled down in front of him, bobbing his pudgy carcass rapidly and with a warm smile splitting his round face nearly in halves.

"Thick steak —" he said, reciting Lewellyn's habitual order, "— one-inch-one-half. Brown spuds. Coffee, plenty sugar. Lin catch quick!"

Steve nodded. The Swede folded a huge slab of ham into his mouth.

"How's Barnage?" he asked around it.

"He'll do," Steve answered. The Swede grunted assent.

"We all will!"

Steve did not answer this. Lin trotted back with Steve's plate. He was hungry. He ate with pleasure. A little traffic moved along the walk outside. It was another day. No different on the surface than those which had preceded it and those which would follow. Both reached a long distance past the horizons of the past and the future. But there was a difference. It was a feeling in Lewellyn.

When he was half through his meal the front door opened and three men filed in out of the sunlight. The first was Sam Dreen, his left arm in a sling and a patch of professional bandaging showing. Apparently McKenna had done his job of stitching. The other two were riders from the camp on the ridge — Willow Creek riders. They had taken seats half a dozen stools up the counter before their eyes adjusted to the interior gloom and they recognized Lewellyn. Steve slowly lowered his fork into his plate and sat motionless. The three slanted their heads together. A word passed from Dreen to the other two. One of these backed from his stool and turned toward the door. Lin barked at the man, his voice thin and high and his accent almost ridiculous, but his intent unmistakable.

"Sitting down! Is wanting breakfast, is getting breakfast!"

The man at the door saw over his shoulder the shortbarreled, undercounter scattergun which Lin had clumsily braced across his hip. He turned slowly back to his seat and sank onto it with a sullen scowl. Lin walked backward to his stove and stood the gun against the wall, near it. At the foot of the counter, beyond Lewellyn, the Swede farmer chuckled with deep pleasure.

Glancing at him, Lewellyn saw the man's belt gun lay in his lap, its hammer eared back in cool readiness. A warmth coursed through Steve. Sharon had talked of her town. She had talked of Brokenbow. But he wondered if she had any knowledge of this kind of friendliness. Harsh, maybe, and violent. But friendliness. The only real nurture the roots of a town could find under freshly turned sod.

Steve finished his meal unhurriedly, left silver beside his plate, and moved toward the door. As he passed behind the three Willow Creek men, Sam Dreen spoke to him.

"We'll be looking for you, Lewellyn!"

"You'll find me, then," Steve said quietly. He pushed the door open.

On the walk, the sun was once more bright in his eyes. He squinted against it. The street was still clear, its shadow and its open marked by clean lines. It seemed likely that Dreen and the two with him were the first down from the Willow Creek camp on the ridge beyond the upper end of the street. He started along the walk toward the two-room store front which was Sock McKenna's office and quarters. As he did so, a man moved out of the deep shadow under the awning of Cragar's mercantile opposite, crossing the walk and stepping down into the dust of the street at an oblique angle. Lewellyn held his pace steady. Ord Keown finished the crossing and stepped up onto the walk beside him in front of an open lot between an empty harness shop and Barnage's store. If he saw Steve's involuntary glance toward the lot behind the store, he gave no sign.

"I've been watching for you, Lewellyn," he said evenly. Steve halted. "Hal Fenton and Sam Dreen swore out a warrant for your arrest this morning."

"And you're serving it, Ord?" Steve asked mildly. Keown's expression did not change.

"It's in my desk," he said. "We'll say I forgot it when I started my rounds —" He broke off and glanced up at the sun. "Nine o'clock. I likely won't get back to my office till noon. That's three hours. If you weren't in town — if you were gone clean when I picked that warrant up — I couldn't serve it."

"I don't suppose," Steve agreed. "Thanks, Ord." The statement was without gratitude. It was a little mocking. Keown's iron grip on duty was slipping. Keown colored a little. An unfamiliar and uncomfortable alteration in the pale changelessness of his complexion.

"Not me, Lewellyn," he said shortly. "No thanks to me. A friend of yours. And I've kept my promise to her. Go or stay. It's the same to me, now!"

Keown swung off and recrossed to the opposite walk. Lewellyn watched him go with a certain admiration. Few men were contained as Keown was. Few men had his strength, his sureness, and his convictions. He had been a little unfair to Sharon, last night. It was more than hunger. Ord Keown, when the shadows were right, could come close to irresistibility. He was legality personified, and as such, stiff and inflexible and maybe reasonless in some things, but he wore his virility with the same vain ease he wore his expensive coats. Steve knew Sharon's metal. He knew her strength as well as her weakness, and he would not belittle it. But she was no match for the marshal of Brokenbow.

Doc McKenna was taking a bath when Steve walked into his dusty office. He had his tub set up in the middle of his reception and consultation room. The floor was pooled with water. The door had not only been unlocked but a little ajar. Sock McKenna had little patience with neatness or modesty for their own sakes. He looked up from rinsing his stocky, vein-knotted body and stood up in his tub, spraying more water carelessly about him.

"Lewellyn!" he grunted. "Might have known somebody would walk in on me. Kick that door shut, will you? There's a draft. You know, I don't mind sleeping in that little two-by-four back room of mine, but damned if I don't have to have a little more space when it's scrub day."

McKenna climbed out of the tub and made wet footprints across the floor to the chair-back where his towel hung.

"I'm a little early," Lewellyn suggested.

"A little!" McKenna snorted. "Hell, you ought to know that in this town it takes half a day for most folks to get moving. Then maybe a couple of hours to decide where they're headed. And by that time the only place left to go is the Grant or the Wagon Wheel or the Spur!"

"You make it sound like Brokenbow's dead."

"It isn't too far from it!" McKenna snapped. "But it'll revive. We'll get a needle into it. We'll make it jump. Can't cure a critter of an ailment till you get it fighting. The madder it is, the quicker it'll heal. Kansas isn't worth a damn to a doctor. Never will be. Too much sun and hard work. Too little time to think about pains and ills. But I've got to where I like the place and I'm tired of moving. So I'll take my practice as it comes and let it go at that. I don't want to see this town roll over and die. And it's apt to. It's got the longhorn plague almighty bad!"

The doctor hauled on his breeches, hooked his suspenders over surprisingly thick shoulders, and started rummaging in his medicine bag. He swore a little as a man will who hunts for something which eludes him. Finally he straightened with a scalpel. Dropping into the only chair in the room, leaving Lewellyn still on his feet by the door, he started to prune the huge corns on his toes. After a little he glanced up sharply at Steve. "There's talk afoot this morning. How much time did Ord give you to clear out?"

"Till noon."

"Um. Three hours. Kind of short. You'll play hell selling your place in that time. Don't suppose you'll go till you've closed a deal on that?"

177

"No," Steve said.

Doc McKenna repeated himself. "Um. Three hours. I didn't figure Ord would do that. No, I didn't, Lewellyn. Not at all. If I was him and you was you, I'd have got me a nice solid place for an arm rest and my best rifle, and I'd have put a thirty-thirty slug through the crown of your hat — from a distance, quiet and comfortable. You've got a mean way of talking back. I laid out that boy you put away in the Grant last night. Two strings and a half inch was all that was holding him together in the middle. But maybe I don't figure Ord as big as he figures himself. Maybe that's a mistake, eh?"

McKenna got up, tossed his scalpel carelessly into his bag, and went into the little back room. He banged the doors open and shut in a tall chest. Finally he turned around, a pair of socks in his hand and his face red with exertion. When he pulled the socks on, the big, crooked great toe of one foot thrust out through a generous hole. He scowled.

"Man without a woman's a confounded baby. Look at that. Sew a rip a mile long in a belly, but I can't close a hole in a sock! Nothing like a good woman — pretty, if you can keep from working her so hard she loses it — a good woman with a little brains and a touch of loyalty. Rounds a man out. Gives him heft he hasn't got alone. Squares off his thinking —"

McKenna paused with a gnomish archness. His obviousness irritated Lewellyn.

"You talking about Zoe?" he said sharply.

"Jed's girl?" McKenna said hurriedly, suddenly all innocence. "So help me, Lewellyn, I didn't know you knew her!"

Steve swore. He had anticipated anger. Instead, he was amused.

"I'm pulling out," he said. "Remember? As soon as my place is sold. Maybe today. Maybe tomorrow. Probably sure the day after."

A wide smile creased McKenna's face, wholly disarming. Lewellyn saw the doctor was relieved. He understood. Jed Barnage was McKenna's friend. Zoe was Jed's daughter. McKenna was taking first things first. Steve grinned in answer. His respect for this red-haired wild man was increasing. McKenna ducked into the back room and came out dragging another chair.

"Sit down, Lewellyn," he invited briskly. "Sure, you're pulling out. Sometime. But nobody knows when. And while you're here, you're up to your ears in trouble, same as everybody else in this town that amounts to a damn. That's why I asked you to come by this morning."

"My trouble is private, McKenna," Lewellyn said steadily.

"The hell!" the doctor grunted. "Trouble is about as private as an outhouse. There are some things we all got to do alike. Now, look. The rest will be along directly. We figure we've all got to pull together. We want to be set when Fenton

179

brings his next drive in here. His crew will be doubled then. He'll be ready to clamp down. We're going to be ready for him."

"I'll be gone when that herd gets here —"

"Sure, sure," McKenna agreed impatiently. "Lewellyn, what do you make of Keown? He bothers me. I know where he stands. But how long can he stand there? Can a man wade a stream when it gets over his head? What we aim to do is set us up a full township government — something we haven't got because everybody's been too busy, so far. We figure on getting us some ordinances. Taking the judgment out of Keown's hands. Giving him a pattern to go by. Can he do it?"

"I don't know. Neither does Ord. Nor anybody else, from here. Depends on what he comes up against. The point is, will he try? I can't tell you, McKenna. Maybe if he thinks your ordinances fit what's needed. Keown's gone a long way on his judgment. He'll probably aim to stick to it."

"He's got to see it our way," McKenna said earnestly. "This isn't a one-man town — good or bad. There's more than one man in it. And we've all got to pull on the same trace. We —"

Lewellyn held up his hand sharply.

"We — ?" he said in challenge.

Almost with the word, a heavy knock sounded on McKenna's street door. The doc rose and started across the room. Midway, he glanced back over his shoulder at Lewellyn and grinned.

180

"Sure. We. You and me and half a dozen others that count!" he said. He reached out and pulled the door open.

Hal Fenton stood on the single step below the sill. Beside him were Sam Dreen and the two riders who had been in Kei Lin's restaurant. The doctor was motionless for a moment, just long enough for the thought to strike Lewellyn that McKenna didn't realize the difference between this and poker. This wasn't a game. The doc didn't have a chance. Also, in this moment, Fenton had time enough to say:

"We want Lewellyn!"

Then McKenna's foot stabbed against the base of the door, hinting purpose, and his squat body blurred into motion. A square red fist cracked audibly against Fenton's jawline, spilling him backward onto the walk. The foot against the door hooked and the door slammed solidly shut. Sock McKenna's hand tumbled the lock over as he dropped. A quick hot volley of shots, three or four, tore into the planking from the outside. McKenna rolled across the floor and onto his feet beside Lewellyn.

"Here we go, boy!" he exulted, and he reached for a dusty rifle in the corner behind him. Lewellyn blinked. The doctor's chances in anything took a sharp upward revision in his mind.

Chapter 8

Lewellyn slid along the wall of Doc McKenna's reception room, his back flat to it, to a place beside one front window. McKenna dodged across to the opposite window. He spoke swiftly, urgently, to Steve.

"Get out through the back room. There's a window there. It'll take them a minute to get their heads and I can hold them a little longer."

Steve shook his head.

"If they want me this bad, they'll have somebody out back, too."

Cautiously he bent until he had a line of vision into the street through a corner of the smudged window. Sam Dreen had a gun in his fist, the muzzle hanging down. One of the riders beside him was punching a spent shell from a chamber. Hal Fenton was standing in the gutter, angrily rubbing his jaw and talking rapidly. From the Spur in one direction and the livery in the other, more Willow Creek men were converging on the doctor's office, most of them jogging in a run. Sam Dreen suddenly put his gun up and took a pane of glass out across the room, a foot from Doc McKenna's belly. The doctor pulled his lips back from his teeth with honest pleasure and began a clumsy swing with his rifle. Lewellyn reached quickly for him with his voice.

"Wait!"

A man was running on the walk, his bootfalls loud in a sudden silence before the office. He came into view in a moment, moving swiftly and without effort. He veered off of the planking and pulled up in front of Hal Fenton.

"What's come off?" he demanded.

Fenton raised his hand toward McKenna's closed door. His voice was tight with anger.

"Lewellyn's in there, Ord!"

Keown swung around to look at the door. He shrugged.

"He has till noon," he said.

Sam Dreen wheeled toward the marshal. "Noon? Hell, who says he does?"

"I say so, Sam," Keown answered steadily. "Noon. That's soon enough."

Dreen pushed forward, holding his bandaged arm clear. Fenton cut in front of him and dropped his hand to Keown's shoulder. Lewellyn could see the bite of Fenton's whitened knuckles.

"It isn't, Ord!"

Keown shook the rancher's grip off. His voice dropped a level in intensity, so that it was barely audible within the office.

"When you're kingpin of Brokenbow, you can say that, Fenton. You can unpin badges and hang them where you like. But as long as I'm afoot behind the one on my vest now, you ride with me! Use your head. You want to smoke

183

Lewellyn out. But you want more than that too. Look up the street. You want to smoke them out too? You ready? You want to tackle the whole job, now?"

Fenton stepped back, turned his head up the street. The angle of the window prevented Lewellyn from following his stare. Fenton stood woodenly for a moment, then swung back on Keown. He scowled.

"All right, Ord. But I've got to talk to you!"

"Sure," Keown smiled easily. "But get this street clear. Send your boys back up to the camp and keep them there. You've got to do a thing the hard way, every time. Use your head, Fenton. Lewellyn's place is for sale. You want grass and you want him on the move. Buy him."

"I offered to once," Fenton said flatly. "Better than three years ago. He told me to go to hell. That's where I'm pointing him now. Nobody's going to buy his place. He'll run barefooted or I'll see him hung!"

Keown shrugged.

"Get your boys moving —"

Fenton snapped an order at the gathering knot of his riders. They began a drift down the street. Keown moved with them and Fenton. As they pulled away from before McKenna's office, another group of men came in from the other direction, walking purposely in the street midway between the planking of the walks. Steve recognized among them Cragar and the fat face of Kinner from the hotel, and Kei Lin. There were more. Three loose ranks. They turned in toward McKenna's door. The doctor saw them from his window and turned back the latch on the door. They trooped into the office without greeting. A dozen grim men with Brokenbow in their hands.

McKenna nodded to each as he came through the door and pushed the door closed when the last had stepped in out of the sun. He turned to Cragar, a little hunched and absently affable with years of tending trade across the counter of a general store.

"You remember everything that's said here, Cragar," McKenna said. "Write it down in some kind of a book when you get back to your place. We got to have a record. We got to have minutes. Jed's abed and will stay there a spell. I'll do his talking and his voting along with mine. The rest of you have got heads and tongues and I hope to hell some backbone! Meeting's to order!"

They settled along the baseboards on the floor, backs to the wall. Some made traceries in the dust on the floor of McKenna's office. Some stared at the outdated collection of calendars hung haphazardly on the walls. Some watched the faces of the others. But each had his brief few words in the next hour. And the best sense came from Kei Lin. What he said had a beginning and an end, with meat between.

"Is fire. Don't want fire, put on water. Want fire, put on coal oil. Lin catch bucket, bring him along. Is water, is coal oil; all the same by Lin."

Listening to some of the others, stumbling and uncertain and trying to trade themselves out of something to which their presence in Brokenbow irrevocably committed them, Lewellyn found his respect for Sock McKenna and the little Chinese restaurant man grow. McKenna blew a trumpet. Kei Lin whispered. But the two of them were alike. There was no middle ground. They bucked Willow Creek Ranch to the limit or they let Hal Fenton take over their town without a breath of protest. Near eleven, Lewellyn straightened where he stood in the doorway of McKenna's rear room.

"There's stock in the corral at my place to be fed and a cow to be milked," he said.

The talk died abruptly. McKenna stood up and crossed to him. For the first time Lewellyn realized the importance to these others of his presence among them. An importance he judged Sock McKenna had carefully planted and nurtured. McKenna was making this difficult for him. Deliberately so.

"We've cut you into this deal of ours even with the rest of us, Lewellyn," McKenna said. "Your cards are no worse than what any of us hold. And maybe you savvy how to play them better than the rest of us. Enough better to know there's got to be wind before a storm. There's got to be talk ahead of anything else. Saving Devore, who wouldn't come in, and Jed Barnage, who couldn't, this is Brokenbow, right here. And you're a part of it."

Lewellyn shook his head.

"You're wrong, McKenna," he said quietly. "This is Brokenbow's stores and Brokenbow's traders. This is the street, the folks in town. But that's only part of it. And I don't belong, I'm off the grass. I'm a farmer. This is the farmer's town, too. When they come in, maybe I'll want a chair — if I'm still here."

"You will be," McKenna said shortly. "You won't sell. Fenton'll see to that. And you've backed water as far as you can. You won't pull out unless you do sell. I can figure you that close. We can't wait for the other farmers. You can't either. Farmers always ride when it's too late, and you know it!"

"I'll watch my own toes," Lewellyn said shortly.

McKenna shrugged but kept his eyes on him in speculation. The townsmen stirred, opening a way for him at the door. Lewellyn stepped into the street. His going was deliberate. Not that he wanted no part of the planning. Not that planning wasn't necessary. But it had been shapeless and overly cautious in his presence, and he understood. The men from the street were afraid of him as they were afraid of all tall men from the south. Afraid of his eyes and afraid of his gun. The three years he had spent among them and his stubborn attachment to his homestead had eased this somewhat, but the dead man he had left lying on Charlie Bissel's floor had brought much of it back. This was, if she could ever realize it, Sharon Devore's strongest argument. This was the compulsion which drove Lewellyn to waiting and patience and trading when the gamut of his instincts dictated swift and decisive action. And he knew himself well enough to realize that he could not make himself a part of Sock McKenna's council without recurrence of the old pattern of thought and action.

His own interests. He had only these to protect. And they did not yet lie in Brokenbow. They were still out on the section of grass Hal Fenton had boasted he would not be able to sell.

As he turned up the walk, Steve saw two riders rise from their haunches under the awning across the front of the Spur. They made no forward move, but they kept their eyes on him steadily. More, he picked up the steady scrutiny from other scattered doorways along the street as he advanced. It began to build up, the surveillance, until it had substance and weight. That not one of the Texans broke was proof of the magic in the voice and their confidence in the gunhand of the marshal of Brokenbow. Keown had strength.

In front of the *Courier* a word halted Lewellyn. "Steve!"

He swung into the shade of the building, lifting his eyes. Sharon stood in the doorway of the office. Her face looked a little harsh in the shadows, although she was frowning deeply with open concern and the harshness might have been in these lines.

"Steve, you're leaving? Your time is running short. . . ."

"Who can stop a clock?" Lewellyn answered.

"You were at the meeting. I saw you leaving McKenna's. What's coming?"

"Ask John," Lewellyn said bluntly. "They approached him."

"John! —" She touched the name with disgust. "I'm not talking about John, I'm talking about you. Steve, you *are* leaving? You *are* getting out? Ord promised. You're not backing McKenna?"

Lewellyn replaced his hat.

"No, I'm on my way up for my horse. Ord kept his promise. You expect thanks for that. Sharon?"

She shook her head.

"Just a promise from you, Steve — that you won't come back. That you'll keep out of this for good. That you'll give Ord his chance to handle it, alone."

"You think he can? I'm sorry, Sharon. I'm making no promises. Maybe I don't owe you as much as Ord does."

Sharon came down one step into the street. She clutched at Steve's arm.

"It means so much, Steve. To me — to the town. You're a lighted match — a flaming match. And we're all walking on powder. More than just men. Women are walking on it too. Kids behind curtained windows. A man's pride isn't that important. A single man isn't — or a dozen of them. Please, Steve. Please go — and stay away!"

A shadow appeared in the doorway above Sharon. Devore's voice reached down.

"Sharon!"

Devore took the step down, seized Sharon, and pulled her roughly up the step. There was sufficient violence in the move to make her stagger a little in the doorway.

"By God, do I have to lock you in the back room twenty-four hours a day to keep you off this street?" he snapped. He swung toward Lewellyn but Steve turned and moved unhurriedly up the walk. He had seen Sharon's eyes. He had seen the harshness in her normally soft and even features crystallize in thin angles. He thought there must be some strain of courage in Devore or he wouldn't deliberately strike that kind of fire from the steel in Sharon.

Ord Keown was standing in the doorway of the post office. He stepped onto the walk as Lewellyn's shadow reached him. He glanced coolly out from under the awning to measure the sun.

"Whittling it a little close, Lewellyn," he observed impersonally. "Your horse is back of the Grant. I had it saddled and brought down for you. No use rubbing more salt across Willow Creek than necessary."

Steve made no answer.

"You going, Lewellyn?"

Steve nodded.

"Where?"

"Out on the grass."

Keown considered this answer. He looked keenly at Steve for a moment, then turned back into the post office. Steve crossed the street, passed down along the side of the Grant, and found his horse. As he rose into the saddle, he glanced back along the building and across the street at the post office. Keown had come back out onto the steps again. He had a couple of pieces of mail in his hand, but his eyes were on Steve. Lewellyn wheeled and rode across broken ground, angling for the toe of the ridge which sheltered his valley and the best graze in the basin.

He envied Keown's icy confidence and Sharon's faith in the four-bit metal stamping on the marshal's tailored vest. It was Sharon who had said justice could never be one man and that no man with a gun could usurp the judgment of God.

Chapter 9

Lewellyn climbed the summit of the rise across the toe ridge back of town and pulled up for a moment. Inevitability was saddlemate with him. He had made his gesture. Fenton had emptied it. There would be no buyer for his grass. He was bound to Brokenbow, then. Held by the principle which had brought him up from La Mesa. Defense of himself and only himself. Because of Sharon, perhaps, if not for her. But because of her or for her, he had limitations. He could sell his land, even under pressure. He could go that far. But he could not be forced from it.

Two breaks to the south, he could see the mouth of Tie Creek. Since he was staying, he thought that in the morning he would get away from his own place early enough to swing south and look at what was left on the Westfall place. He had not known the dead man well. But he had been a neighbor, geographically at least. And something would have to be done for Westfall's woman. She had three or four kids. He wasn't sure of the count. They had to be fed. More than that, they had to have a house of their own and something toward which they could look as they grew. Kids needed such an anchor for a fair start. The Tie Creek land was good.

Something would come out of it. Likely Jed Barnage would already have a plan.

A smoke finished, Lewellyn swung north and west from the summit, going into the cut of a little creek. He traveled the course of this a pair of miles, then turned against a transverse rise, aiming to come out above his own house. There was a road of sorts up the big valley, but this way was quicker and held to timber for the most part, making a cooler ride in the full sun. Dropping down the far side of the last ridge toward the timber fringe above the grass of the valley, Lewellyn came suddenly on another rider. The man raised his hand in greeting.

"Howdy, neighbor," he called.

Lewellyn pulled up. This Swede farmer had a way of being in many different places. Steve eyed him curiously. The Swede grinned. He turned toward a break through the timber. Lewellyn's square shack was visible through it, a pair of miles down the slope.

"Got a little company down there," the Swede said. "Thought you might like to know. Don't care about riding into surprise parties, myself. Not that kind!"

"No," Steve agreed. The Swede stood at his horse's head, looking up. Steve swung down. "We seem to travel about the same speed," he told the Swede. "Reckon we ought to know each other."

The Swede put out a thick, corded hand. "I like to call my neighbors' names," he admitted.

"I'm Christoffersen. I'm proving up that quarter above the slough between here and Tie Creek. That is, I've filed on it. Seems maybe like fencing might go a little slow in the basin for a spell. More men than land — or maybe it's too much beef —"

"Who's down below, Christoffersen?"

"To the point, eh?" The Swede grinned. "I'm a mite nervous myself. It's like this. I'm new. I don't know many folks. They didn't invite me to their meeting this morning, and after Keown backed those drovers off of the street it looked quiet for a spell, so I started back out to my place. Your company overhauled me two-three miles out. I was in the bush when they went by. Sam Dreen was riding point in the bunch and it didn't look too good, so I trailed them. We could cut back over the ridge and bed down at my place tonight."

Lewellyn shook his head impatiently.

"Dreen and who else?"

"Three more. That white-haired kid they call Curly. Don't know the names of the others. The Willow Creek outfit's getting too big in here to keep them all spotted."

Lewellyn looked out through the timber into his own meadow. His face was expressionless.

"Thanks, Christoffersen," he said. "I'll drift your way when the chance comes. But I'm on my way out from town for my chores now. Reckon I'd better tend to them."

The Swede snorted.

"Hell, what you think I've been sitting here two hours for? Just to see the color of your eyes? Look, one of their horses isn't hid worth a damn down there. You'd have spotted it a long time before you rode in on them. No need for me to wait just to warn you. No need for you to try cheating me out of sampling your company either! I don't get any, down my way."

Lewellyn laughed. The devil rode a high horse behind this man's unhurried exterior. Steve remounted. Christoffersen swung up also. They circled together with the timber fringe, holding their level on the slope above the grass until they were behind the house below. Here thick, uncleared brush reached down almost to its walls. They left their horses two hundred yards into the timber and worked on afoot. Reaching the rear wall of the house, they angled to the left, going around the windowless north end. From here they could see the four horses, tied close in a berry thicket beyond Steve's makeshift corral.

"One'll be in the barn," Christoffersen murmured. "I'll make for him. Just sit tight. If he rackets, the others'll jump and you'll have to keep them off my back if you can. If he don't — and I don't reckon he will if I run to luck at all — I'll be back directly and we'll have better odds."

Steve nodded. The Swede drifted away, going through the brush without guile, but using a prudent man's caution. He made a bad job of crossing the little creek which watered the corral and Steve flattened against the corner of the house, his eyes on the front door. The noise drew two men who had been within the shadows of the doorway. They stood motionless in the sun, blinking a little and listening. One of them spoke shortly.

"That damned milker! She's about to bust —"

"Let her!" his companion snapped. "Damn it, this gets itchy. I'd rather pick Lewellyn up along the trail. Never did like another man's house when I wasn't invited!"

Sam Dreen's voice came irritably from behind the two in the doorway, from somewhere within the house.

"Along the trail, Miller?" Dreen asked. "You wouldn't if you knew all they tell about Lewellyn. You wouldn't if you'd ever seen him work. I have."

Dreen paused. In a moment he continued.

"Never give a man like that room to work in or you'll be sorry. He won't expect to find us here. We'll have him hocks down the minute he hits the door. If we miss it, Curly'll drop him from the barn. Sit it tight, boys. It won't be long. A farmer doesn't let a fresh cow like that one in the barn go very far past noon without milking. There's cigars in here. I found a box. Have one."

One of the two in the doorway turned back into the room. The other stepped on out into the sun and surveyed the slopes above. The first followed him out in a moment, holding one of Steve's long tobacco rollers in his hands. He

196

spoke over his shoulder to Dreen, still within the house.

"Too black for me, Sam. But Curly likes his strong. It's quiet above. I'll take it across to the barn and see if Curly's set."

Dreen grunted an answer. The man swung across the yard at a light, quick pace. Lewellyn stiffened a little and slid his gun free. He judged Christoffersen would reach the barn seconds ahead of the man in the yard. The Swede's attention would be ahead of him. He would be coming up on the barn doors with his back open. It wouldn't do. Lewellyn stood up full, levelled his gun to a fine sight, and fired.

The man in the yard, the one who had been called Miller, he thought, spun with a frightened yelp and went down heavily. Dreen and the other drover were just inside the door, close enough to the open to know where the shot had come from. They drove into the open, wheeling toward him together. The drover was a pace ahead, his gun down for a low shot. Steve fired again without care, driving the man limply backward into Dreen. At the same time he said:

"Easy, Sam!"

Dreen wavered, drew tight, and raised his good hand slowly. When it was at the limit of his reach, he opened his fingers and let his gun fall. Steve crossed, pushed Dreen against the side of the house, and crouched beside him. The door of the barn swung out with slow caution, making a black square of shadow in the side of the

197

building, into which a man couldn't see. When the sag of the door made its bottom scrape on dirt and stopped its swing, a man came out. A big, grinning man who dragged another behind him.

"In a hurry, eh, Lewellyn?" Christoffersen called reproachfully. Steve turned his head toward the drover he had dropped in the yard. Christoffersen followed the look. Miller had rolled to his knees. His hands were clamped tightly around one thigh. The Swede angled across to him and lifted his gun. Straightening, he put his foot to Miller's shoulder and rolled him again into the dust.

"Lie down!" he growled. "When we want you up, we'll whistle!"

Sam Dreen hacked and spat. Lewellyn looked at him and spoke softly.

"You should have left this to Keown, Sam. It takes a badge to serve a warrant."

"Who said anything about a warrant?" Dreen snapped. "I had my orders."

"Hal's tallied me off? Why — because of that hand that checked out in the Grant last night?"

Dreen grinned thinly.

"Hell, no. Did Hal tally you off for Randee, down in La Mesa? Or Banta or Les Macambridge? He's had too many hands shot off his payroll, Lewellyn. It's grass again. Hal wants this basin. He's got an idea it won't come easy with you hanging around. He just wants to shorten the odds. That's all. You should have let Keown serve you in town this morning — or made him do it. You'd have both been better off!"

Lewellyn made no answer. Dreen watched him keenly for a moment, then he shrugged and moved off toward the creek at the corral. Christoffersen loosened his hold on the collar of the man he had dragged from the barn. The man's head dropped into the dust, making a puddled mess in his hair where the blood had welled from a gash at the back of his part. The Swede's eyes followed Dreen.

"You letting him ride back to town alone?" he asked Lewellyn. Steve shook his head.

"No. The rest go with him. Two can sit their saddles when he's sloshed them with water. He can tie the other one on crossways. I want my yard clean."

Christoffersen scowled.

"I had a notion I'd like to ride into Brokenbow with the whole damned crew strung out behind me. I figured I'd enjoy watching Keown's face when we turned them over to him for his lockup. Maybe he'd put his heels down a little heavier if we did. I don't like a lawman that walks so light."

"Uh-uh," Steve said flatly. "I know these boys. I've ridden with their kind. Pride grows tall in north Texas. They'll take a beating at even odds or better. But they won't be bullied, and they won't take salt where they're hurt. Dreen can ride in like this and it won't run to personalities. A sour chore. A rotten run of luck. The rest of Willow Creek will take it for that. But Ord

Keown and a company of cavalry couldn't keep us from being shot out of our saddles if we rode into town with this bunch tied in a string behind us."

"You hinting we'd ought to stay out of town, anyways?"

"It'd be smart," Lewellyn agreed.

Christoffersen shook his head. "Not me!" he said decisively.

Dreen came back up from the creek with water in his hat. He got the man from the barn up on his feet. He got Miller up from the dust. The wounded drover swore at the hurt in his leg and crawled into his saddle with a deal of effort. Dreen and the man from the barn lifted the dead man out of the dooryard of the house. They spilled him on his belly across his saddle and tied him on. The four horses strung out of the yard. Lewellyn watched them into the timber before turning back to the house. His rifle was in its scabbard over the mantel. He took it down and carried it outside. The Swede came down the slope with their horses. Steve thrust the rifle into its scabbard and turned down toward the corral where the cow with the full udder was bawling again. Christoffersen followed him. A battered bucket was inverted over one of the posts holding the bars of the corral gate. Lewellyn took it down. Christoffersen leaned against the bars. Lewellyn saw he was grinning.

"I'll wait for you," Christoffersen said. "I guess we're both damned fools."

Chapter 10

Christoffersen and Lewellyn came in by the valley road, winding around the edge of the ride and into the upper end of the street. The town was strangely quiet, the street empty. They racked their ponies in front of Jed Barnage's hardware store and stood on the walk. It took a little time to recognize the change in the town and its cause. Finally Lewellyn's eyes raised to the slope beyond the head of the street, back of them as they had ridden in. The sprawl of the huge, untidy Willow Creek camp was gone. Only an irregular patch of litter on the grass remained. Lewellyn frowned. He glanced at Christoffersen. The Swede had seen also. Christoffersen scrubbed the knuckles of one big hand against his cheek.

"I need a drink!" he finally decided aloud.

Lewellyn did not move. Christoffersen waited a moment for him, then stepped down from the walk and cut toward the Grant. As he reached the other walk Ord Keown came out of the Spur, saw Lewellyn, and started across. Christoffersen wheeled and followed him back, stopping a pair of yards behind him. Christoffersen had said out on the grass that he didn't like Keown. That dislike showed in his eyes, now. Keown stood in the gutter, one foot up on the walk in front of Steve. The skin about his eyes was without color. His nostrils flared a little with each breath and his breathing seemed more rapid than usual. Rapid and shallow. There was a slight sway to his body, like the restlessness of a cat. Lewellyn thought the man was under strain. He wondered about it.

"It's a long time past yesterday noon, Lewellyn," Keown said quietly.

Steve nodded, waiting. Keown said nothing for a long moment, his eyes steadily on Lewellyn's face.

"So what am I going to do, Lewellyn — is that it?" he murmured.

"Something like," Steve agreed. Keown's eyes narrowed.

"Not what I want to. Not what I'd like to," he said. "My hands are tied. Hal Fenton came down and tore up his warrant for you before he rode out with his crew."

Lewellyn was startled.

"Why?" he asked carefully. Keown shrugged.

"Because trouble's done," he said sharply. "The whole thing was smoke over a brush pile. It could have been worse. You and your long nose in everybody else's business could have made it worse. But patience pays off, Lewellyn. It pays to stand still and feel the wind."

"Some winds can blow a man down, Ord," Steve suggested. "— When he stands alone —"

Keown nodded. He smiled briefly.

"But that wind didn't blow —" he said.

There was a kind of relief in his voice. Suddenly Steve understood. He understood Keown and his jumpiness and the stubbornness which made him attempt to carry the peace of Brokenbow on his shoulders alone. He had talked with Sharon. He had talked with Sharon as Steve had once talked to her. Sharon's mark was on him also. Steve wondered if Pete Lynch's daughter would ever understand that a woman could destroy a man as easily as she could build him. He wondered if she would ever see that peace was not only a concept of the heart, but something physical too, made up of men and movement and angers and judgments, both good and bad.

He saw now that Keown had been afraid when the Willow Creek crew had been in town. He had been afraid of McKenna and his meetings. Not cowardice, but the practicality of his nature measuring the odds of the forces piling against him. Honest fear, for which a man was to be respected. Keown had been afraid. Maybe he even knew the complete folly of his singlehanded play — the impossibility of restraining either faction in the town if a spark flew. And his jumpiness now was half self-condemnation and half relief. A reaction.

"You couldn't have done it, Ord," Steve said quietly. "Your star would have been the first target. Fenton will be back. Don't try it again. Don't try it alone. That isn't what she wants. She doesn't want you dead."

The white under Keown's eyes spread to the crown of his cheeks.

"Damn you, Lewellyn, mind your own business!" he snapped. He wheeled to move briskly away, but Christoffersen, close behind him on wide-planted legs and with strong interest in his eyes, partially blocked his path. Without intent, Lewellyn knew. But he was there. Tight with anger, Keown was startled. He bore angrily ahead instead of side-stepping Christoffersen's bulk. The Swede fended him off with a clumsy thrust of his big hand. The touch seemed to loose something in the smaller man. Keown did a rash thing. With sickening ease, he slid a gun from his belt and wiped its barrel savagely at Christoffersen's head.

Startled, the Swede avoided the stroke, and a swift pleasure came up in his eyes. His big body swung with astonishing swiftness. The corded hands caught hold so fast they made sharp, snapping sounds. Keown's gun sailed out into the street. Christoffersen spun him effortlessly, caught him again by the front of his coat, and smashed his free hand against Keown's jaw. Ord dropped where he stood. The Swede stepped over him and grinned at Steve. Lewellyn grabbed his arm.

"Get down to McKenna's and stay there, out of sight!" he said rapidly. "I owe you something. This is it."

Christoffersen, still grinning satisfaction,

started to protest. Steve drove his words at him hard.

"Get off the street, quick!"

The fun died in Christoffersen's eyes. He glanced down at the man in the gutter. Turning, he walked rapidly up the walk toward McKenna's office. Lewellyn stepped down and dragged Keown onto the walk. The man was iron. He stirred, already shaking off the impact of the Swede's heavy blow. Steve held him down. His eyes opened, bottomless and unreadable. Men were tumbling across from Whisky Row. Steve held Keown down a moment longer, then straightened and backed away. If Christoffersen hadn't slowed, he would now be out of sight at McKenna's. Keown got unsteadily to his feet and dusted himself. The men coming across saw his face and abruptly changed their direction. He spoke to Steve in a small, metal-thin voice.

"Don't ever corner me again, Lewellyn!" he warned. He turned away. Steve watched him along the walk until he stepped into his own office. The mail wagon came up from the depot. Steve followed it, remembering that it had been a week since he had opened his box at the post office.

There was no mail for him. Ruth Barnage was at the express window, struggling with a box plastered with the stickers of a mail-order house in Kansas City. Steve lifted it down for her. She smiled at him.

"Thanks, Steve. Big night at our place. I got one of them pant-legged pajama suits in here for Jed. Says his gowns crawl up on him and his leg gets cold at night since he got it hurt. Never figured I'd sleep with a man that had his pants on, but when Jed gets an idea there's nothing more to it!" Barnage's wife laughed. "Pick it up and come along, Steve. Zoe had a roast on when I came up town. It'll be fair eating. And there's a dress in here for her. She'll want to show it, sure."

"I came in to see Sock McKenna," Steve answered.

Ruth Barnage laughed again. "Nonsense! Never ate with Doc, did you? Well, don't. Besides, Jed heard you had a little talk with Sam Dreen today. He'll want to know about that. And our door locks as tight as any in town. Come along!"

Lewellyn lifted the box and followed Ruth through the door. The Barnage women were compelling. Out on the street Ruth got a good hold on his free arm, talking eagerly. As they came abreast the *Courier* office, Sharon jumped up from a table within and ran to the door.

"Hello, Mrs. Barnage," she said, stopping Ruth's flow of talk. "I want to see you, Steve —"

Ruth Barnage nodded brightly. "Good. Come up to the house tonight, Mrs. Devore. Steve'll be there. Bring the Mister. Jed likes company —"

Sharon glanced helplessly at Steve. He grinned and raised his brows. John Devore came

206

down to the window of the office and glowered out at the walk. Sharon turned wordlessly back inside. Ruth Barnage stared at Sharon's departing back with a little sag of hurt about her lips. She shrugged and started forward again.

"She won't come," Ruth said flatly, with certain knowledge. "She's never been in my parlor. Nor anybody else's I know of. She's a beautiful thing. I feel sorry for her husband."

Lewellyn was startled. Even considering the night behind Jed's store, Devore had never struck him as a man worthy of anything like the rich sympathy on tap in the comfortable woman beside him. And Ruth could not know anything about the weeds of back lots. She was as wide as this country, and the narrow and twisting channel of John Devore's life should have been a thing beyond her understanding. His surprise was in his eyes. Ruth saw it.

"That man was made for working with his hands. He was made for a plain woman with a soft voice and flat feet," she said firmly. "This one is too much for him. And he can't answer enough in her, either. That's a bad thing, Steve. That's what makes marrying different than breeding cows. Mismatching don't bring good. I'm sorry for Sharon Devore too. She's a good woman."

Lewellyn thought there was a curious little emphasis on Ruth's last phrase. He glanced quickly at her. Her eyes were somber.

"This is a little town, Steve. There isn't much

that happens in it that somebody doesn't know. And sometimes it takes a lot of thinking to get the right slant on things. You sure you're thinking right — about Mrs. Devore and Ord Keown?"

Ruth paused. Lewellyn made no comment.

"A man seldom does on a thing like that," Ruth went on thoughtfully. "Aren't many men that know a woman. I doubt if you do, and you're big enough. It's time you did. There are some women who have to have a strong current close enough so they can hear it, all the time — like a river. The Lord knows there's a strong stream in Ord Keown, Steve. I hope Sharon Devore don't get washed off her feet. Ord gets his strength from washing over rocks. She needs deeper water. It'd be better for both, some other way."

Ruth fell silent. Lewellyn picked up her thought about the currents of men and turned it in his mind, inwardly making personal application. He was still engaged in this when they reached the house. Zoe met them at the door. She had her heavy hair up on top of her head. The heat of the kitchen had flushed her face. Excitement brightened in her eyes when she saw him. She reached her hand out to him unconsciously, pulling at his arm. Her mother took her mail-order box from him, glanced knowingly at the two of them, and moved off briskly into the back hall, leaving Zoe and Lewellyn alone within the front door.

"For supper, Steve?" Zoe asked hopefully.

"Your mother says so," Steve agreed.

"And I thought it was too hot a day to cook a roast! Dad's in the parlor. Go talk to him. I've got to fuss . . ."

Zoe turned away, then swung back, her head tilted a little.

"Been thinking about the grass, Steve?" she asked.

"A little," Steve admitted non-committally.

"You can tell me about it — after supper —" Zoe turned and ran back through the house, calling for her mother. Lewellyn stood in the doorway for a moment, thinking that there could be a great many changes between one night and the next — even between a man and a woman. He tried to discover what was missing for him in Zoe Barnage.

Maybe she was like the land. Rich in harvest or poor by the whim of nature. Always demanding of time and labor. There was the filing and the moving in and the living. There were the improvements. In the end it belonged to him. Maybe it was this way with Zoe. He knew her, talked with her, made his friendships with her family. In time they'd marry. And she would belong to him, like the land.

Lewellyn had owned thoughts about many women. He had looked at many. There were memories of the touch of some. A few who were soft and a few who were hard. But there had been excitement in them all. A kind of game in which a man gambled his pride and his desire against coquetry and beauty; winning or losing as his luck ran. This, he thought, was what lay between Zoe and himself. There was no gamble for Jed Barnage's daughter. There was no lift which sprang from never knowing what lay behind her eyes. He wondered if Jed had found Ruth like this. He thought it was possible. And when he had thus marked the barrier which separated him from Zoe, he knew he had lied to himself. It was not sureness. It was not even Zoe. It was Sharon Devore. He opened a door before him and stepped into the Barnage parlor.

Jed was on the settee. Jennie Westfall sat across the room from him, her youngest child on her knees. She had been crying. She was crying. She made no pretense of hiding her tears. She stood up, gave Steve a little smile, and went out toward the back of the house. Jed waved his hand brusquely.

"There's a bottle in back of the Bible on that stand, Steve. Drag it out. Always gets me when a good woman thinks somebody has given her more than her due!"

Lewellyn found the bottle and a pair of small glasses. Jed poured out two tall ones, set them down, and stared at them speculatively. Steve waited for him. Directly he pushed one toward Steve, lifted the other, and cut it in halves.

"A woman that'll marry a man and come west of the River with him — a woman that'll raise him some clean-nosed kids and keep his house and make him think he's done right by her — that kind of a woman'll never get all that's coming to her. Ain't too much we can do for Jennie. What we can do don't call for the blessings and carryings-on she's been pouring out. Hell, Steve, we've got to see her kids and others like 'em is raised right so they'll be fit to run this country for us when we get too old!"

Lewellyn lifted his own glass. "How much did you give her, Jed?" he asked quietly.

Barnage looked hurt. "Money? Steve, money would have broke her heart. She'd have gotten out of this basin if she had to walk and drag the kids behind her on a cart if I'd have offered her money. I put her to work at the counter in my store. I give her the tool house out back. It was the best I could do. She'll get by in it. Come spring, if winter trade is decent, maybe we can do something about a new house for her out on Tie Creek — all of us."

"I reckon," Steve agreed. He finished his drink. He had left the *llanos* with a conviction that Texas had flint, but it also had its heart, big as the boundaries of the short grass. He had learned much in the three years he had been rooting in Kansas soil. And he thought now that this hardware man — whom he had believed he knew better than any in Brokenbow — was still much a stranger to him.

Zoe came in the door. "It's on!" she said.

Lewellyn rose slowly, hardly realizing that it was the supper to which she referred. She was in her new dress. It clung to her from shoulder to hip. A brick-red sheathing which belled out into a thick, rustling skirt. Lewellyn glanced swiftly at Jed to see if Zoe's father realized what she had done. Only pride was in Jed's eyes. Lewellyn returned his attention to Zoe, to the dress. The mold of her thighs, her flat belly, the out-thrust firmness of her breasts — even the nipples — were accentuated. She stood carefully to make them so. Proudly. Only the honesty in her eyes, only a knowledge that she did not understand fully the effect and the impression, made it possible for Steve to avoid distaste.

There was nothing new in what Zoe had done with this dress. Women from the gaudier cribs and the saloons of most cattle towns had long discovered the directness in their trade. A dress was a necessity of convention. The trick was to make it as unnecessary as possible. A thing generally accomplished by leaving off all other garments which customarily were worn beneath it. Such a skin-tight sheathing had before discounted many a blemish and sagging line. But it hid no other modesty.

Zoe turned and led the way back into the dining room. Muscles rippled under the dress. Steve thought he caught a shadow of a tiny dimple on her hip. He felt uncomfortable. Ruth was already at the table. She eyed Zoe's approach uncertainly, but her eyes were for the most part on Steve. A scrutiny showing evidence of mild shock, perhaps, but loyalty and the eternal conviction of Ruth's kind that all which occurred within the sacred precincts of her home was Godly. A conventional sop to a conscience troubled by many curious events in the course of a lifetime.

Lewellyn stumbled a little in seating himself opposite Zoe and he was sharply aware that his color was high. Ruth smiled; finally she chuckled.

"I figured that dress would do the trick," she said to no one in particular. "I could tell, just looking at it in the catalogue."

Jed laughed with what Steve thought was unnecessary heartiness. He rubbed his nose.

"Never knowed a woman who savvied all like Ruth," he said. "Now, when we've gone fish-ing —"

Suddenly flushed, Zoe pointed to the roast.

"You want the crust, Steve, or do you like yours rare?" she asked.

Chapter 11

The meal was difficult for Lewellyn. So much had passed through his mind since the night before in the arbor with Zoe. So much which would be difficult to lead Zoe through. Yet he knew he owed it to her. At least enough for understanding. And it would be so different from what she expected. With the night before fresh in memory and recollections yet inflammatory — with this dress and her planning, it would be difficult for Zoe to understand that another woman and another woman's body was between them. It would be difficult for any woman to understand. Yet her understanding would have to go beyond this. To the realization that Lewellyn could not be bound by a plow and a fence and a bed. He required subtler chains and a freedom she could not grant.

It was with relief that he heard Sock McKenna's voice at the door while they were still at table. McKenna, asking for him.

"Is Steve Lewellyn here?"

Steve pushed back, starting for the porch, but McKenna's voice drew away.

"Good! Then we'll come up here. Tell Jed."

Jennie Westfall had answered the knock. She met Steve in the dining room doorway.

"It was Doc. A meeting of some kind, I guess. They wanted you, Mr. Lewellyn. Doc said he'd bring the rest along up here."

Jed rubbed his hands together eagerly. "They better not leave me out of this!"

Zoe caught Steve's eye. Regret clouded her own. Unable to do otherwise, he smiled at her, grudgingly making a promise for later. She got up to help her mother with the clearing of the table. Jed rose and hobbled inexpertly on a crude crutch into the parlor. Steve followed. He had just finished propping Jed comfortably on the settee when the hall door swung inward. The men of Brokenbow filed into the room.

It was in the main the same crowd who had been at McKenna's in the morning. There were, however, notable additions. Alex Christoffersen was one, his eyes reaching across to Lewellyn in friendliness. Hal Fenton was another, his face impassive and his eyes very quick. The last was Ord Keown. The whiteness was still present under his eyes and there was an electric sensitiveness in his movements. Like a razor honed to too fine an edge.

Surveying the others, Steve felt the heaviness of inevitability. This was the showdown. And every man present knew it. That Willow Creek was gone from the ridge meant nothing. That Keown, on the street, had claimed it was all over meant nothing also. It was just the beginning. Fenton sat down uncomfortably on a straight chair by the door. He glowered at McKenna and

Keown in turn, then swung on Jed.

"This wasn't my idea, Barnage," he said bluntly. "But I'll go half way with anybody, so I came."

"It's not hard to meet a man who'll come that far, Fenton," Jed said pleasantly. He turned to Doc McKenna. "How far has our side gone, Sock?"

McKenna scowled uncomfortably. "Well, now, Jed, I didn't measure," he said. "Suppose we let Fenton swing his end, and then we'll see how we fit?"

Cragar had an inventory book across his knees and a chewed length of pencil. He scrubbed the canvas cover of the book with his knuckles.

"That's best, Jed," he offered mildly.

Barnage looked at the boss of Willow Creek. Fenton shrugged.

"All right. I moved my crew out this afternoon. Why? To meet my next herd, about eighty miles down the trail. They'll be in the day after tomorrow. This has got to be all quiet, then. We have got to have the pot all counted and split. There've been some bad dogs between us. I'd as soon as the next leave 'em lie!"

Ord Keown was watching Fenton with a peculiar fixity. The rest of the room was tense. There had been speculation about Fenton. There had been rumor. This was fact.

"I need the grass from Tie Creek across the slough and the main ridge to the upper end of the basin," Fenton went on steadily. "I'll buy the

216

homesteads that are there — with one exception —" he paused and glanced sharply at Lewellyn "— at a reasonable price. But I've got to think it's reasonable. And there'll be no new claims filed. My boys will want what they've got money to buy on Whisky Row and among the floozies in the Gulch across the tracks with no hands laid on them. The rest of it is yours and I want none of it."

Jed Barnage swung his head slowly. "Your place is at the top of the big valley, Steve. Will you sell?"

"You heard Hal," Lewellyn answered quietly. "I'm out of this."

"Yours is the one he won't buy?" Jed asked. "All right, for now. Are you getting off of it till you are bought?"

Steve shook his head. Jed nodded at Christoffersen.

"I don't sell. Not for cattle, money or women. I stay." Christoffersen's jaw set stubbornly. Jed sighed and began to drum his fingers on the arm of the settee.

"There's another homestead on that grass you want, Fenton. Westfall's. I'll listen to price."

"I already made an offer on that, Barnage," Hal Fenton said. "A dollar an acre."

Jed sighed again. "Jennie Westfall's here in my house. She wouldn't make a move without my advice. I'd have to tell her that the price wasn't right. All that land you want is open to homestead patent. It'll graze stock, all right, but with the sod turned under it's better land than when the grass is up. Your herds don't make Brokenbow grow. Homesteaders on the slopes do. With a crop in, a section on the ridge would make a sizable family a nice living. A section wouldn't fat one herd for you. You're asking too much!"

"I've got thirty riders!" Hal Fenton said.

Doc McKenna answered him. "We've got a town!"

Fenton stood up. "We can't both win," he said. "One of us has got to lose."

"I'll give you two-to-one on Brokenbow!" Doc McKenna snapped. Fenton pulled open the door and stepped into the hall. A moment later the front door of the house slammed shut behind him. Keown also stood up. His eyes were narrowed.

"How so many damned fools could get together in one place —" he said savagely, and he started for the door. McKenna caught his arm.

"Wait a minute, Ord!" he said. "You've got a part in this. When you came in here, you were told to keep the town quiet. Nobody had time to tell you anything else. The town didn't need anything else. It's different now. And you've been paid regular. From here on you're going to earn it."

McKenna swung on Cragar and reached for the inventory book. Cragar surrendered it. McKenna flipped it open and handed it to Keown.

"We've been making us some laws, Ord," he continued. "This is them. This is the way we want our town run."

Keown scanned the first page, his lips moving. He jerked his head up after a moment and snapped the book closed.

"You think you can peg a bull with a piece of red string? You think you can pour powder on a fire to put it out? This is crazy, McKenna! The worst thing! Extending the town limits so I've got to watch trespass on the slopes. A curfew for the Gulch and Whisky Row! You've got a chance to make a deal with Fenton and you pull this!"

"You think you can't make these ordinances stick, Ord?" Jed Barnage asked gently.

"Think!" Keown's voice came up in pitch. "How much can one man do? I've kept your town quiet. No shooting — till you and Lewellyn horned in with Westfall instead of letting him drink his grudge out and go home stiff with whisky instead of a couple of bullets in his gut! By God, Barnage, marshaling in a town isn't like running a store. When I hike my prices up and things get tough, it isn't the trade falls off. My customers start fighting!"

With a peculiarly animal-like gesture, Keown swung his eyes from the face of one man in the room to another. When he had made the circuit, he spoke again. Softly.

"I've kept Brokenbow quiet. Quiet enough so you all could do your business and sleep with your doors unlocked. Quiet enough for your

219

women to go after your mail and your kids to buy candy in the stores. I'll go on keeping it quiet. But my way, by hell! There's a middle road in anything. That's the one I ride!"

Keown pivoted on his heel, dragged open the door, and strode out of the room. Lewellyn stirred restlessly under the prodding of a strange impression. He had just heard Sharon Devore talk to Brokenbow. Reasonless, impassioned, and half right. Theory and principle and impracticability. Justice and injustice at a compromise for a result a man could not hold in his hand — peace. This was the measure of Ord Keown's devotion. It revealed depths Lewellyn had not thought the marshal of Brokenbow possessed.

The door remained open after Keown stepped through it. After a moment Jed Barnage nodded toward it and spoke to Kei Lin.

"Shut the door —"

The Chinese crossed the room. In the doorway Kei Lin made some gesture and spat almost silently into the outer hall.

"Sock," Jed said patiently to McKenna, "we didn't get far."

"Hell, Jed, we didn't try!" McKenna protested. "You can't chase a skunk with a stick without him stinking you up. When you go after him, he's got to be nailed before he can swing his tail toward you. Look, I wasn't hunting Lewellyn up here a few minutes ago just to see if he'd shaved today. Ord don't like our rules. This is where Steve comes in —"

Zoe was in the arbor. Sitting on the bench with her knees up under her chin and the new dress a pool of color around her. Lewellyn stopped a yard away, bracing himself and reaching for the swiftest words which would not hurt. But Zoe was faster than his mind. She came off the bench in a quick movement, took a step, and threw herself against him, her face upturned. Steve could feel her body through the thin fabric under his hands and it seemed best to begin gently. He kissed her.

There was no thawing preliminary, no conventional gesturing to mask desire. Zoe was youth. Zoe was hunger. Zoe was a woman with only a new dress over her naked body. Lewellyn felt both kindled and a fool, in spite of himself, when Zoe freed him and backed away a moment later. She dropped down onto the bench, more conserving what was in her than restraining it. She tipped her head toward the house.

"What did they want of you, Steve?"

"To listen, mostly."

"Ma says they intended to give Ord Keown his orders tonight. Did he take them?"

"No."

"Then you're the new marshal of Brokenbow!"

Steve sat down a foot away from her along the bench.

"Do you want that?"

Zoe considered this a moment. "Yes. Yes,

Steve, I think I do. I didn't at first. There seemed some other way. But now it looks different. Like the bullet in dad's leg. It could have been left. The wound would have swelled, got infected. Maybe it would have come out by itself. Maybe dad would have lost his leg — or his life. It hurt like the very devil and it was bloody work for Doc McKenna to go in after it with a knife. But maybe the hurt wasn't as much in the long run, and it was over quickly — done with. It's healed fast since. I think our trouble with drovers is like that, I think you could handle the knife."

"And afterward?"

"Our farm, Steve. We can't have it till this trouble is settled. Our white house and our picket fence. Our kids —"

Zoe broke off. She was looking into Lewellyn's face. Suddenly she reached across and turned one of his hands upward. Her fingers traced across his palm. It was a hard hand, muscled and corded. But the fingers were long, flexible, and the skin of palm and finger pads was not thickened and horny with the constant wear of the soil.

"That's what I mean by afterward, Zoe," Steve said gently. "A gun makes few calluses. That's what it would be afterward — Steve Lewellyn, the gunman who quieted Broken-bow."

Zoe exhaled a long, slow breath. "Then that's what it was. That's what you were running away from when you first came here. The shadow of your own gun. And ma said it was likely a woman!"

"That, too. It looks like I didn't go quite far enough to get away from either."

"Then I haven't offered enough?" Zoe's voice was unsteady. Steve closed his fingers on her hand.

"More than any man has a right to," he said softly. "I think that's the trouble. I haven't enough to match it. This kind of a trade has to be even. I can't cheat you. I've wanted to, if that means anything. I've wanted to like hell — a kind of want I'm not used to. Maybe even a kind I've never had before. But I can't."

Zoe had pulled her knees up under her chin again.

"Thanks, Steve — for that, at least —" she murmured.

Steve rose. There were more words, he supposed. But he didn't know where they fitted. He replaced his hat, stooped, and stepped out of the arbor. Half way down the path to Barnage's stable, Doc McKenna stepped out of the shadows and fell in beside him. When they reached the poles of Barnage's tiny corral, Doc halted and produced two cigars. He thrust one at Steve.

"Mosquitoes," he said shortly. "Nothing like a black roll to drive them off."

Steve nodded agreement with this and took the cigar. When the match flared, there was nothing in McKenna's face which could be read.

He was silent for a long time. Finally he spoke again.

"You shouldn't have turned us down tonight, Lewellyn," he said thoughtfully. "Your thinking is wrong. When I was in the army, I got to be somewhat rough in my trade. Butchering in a field hospital with round shot knocking hell out of everything around you can make a doctor a pretty cool customer about the amount of hurting he has to do to get his work done in a hurry. When the war was over, I started hunting a practice. But every so often, when I was just getting well started, there'd be a gent along I'd taken an arm off or a leg or dug a chunk of iron out of, and he'd remember I'd blamed near killed him.

"Those stories got out. Folks would back off. I'd leave, move on. Got clear to Brokenbow, finally, before I come to realize I did a tolerable job and the way I did it was me. Folks would just have to get used to it. So I've stuck here. And I don't starve."

"You'd go back to the army and the army kind of doctoring again if there was another war?" Steve asked. "Is that it?"

McKenna flung his cigar down. "You see what I mean — yes, Lewellyn, I would!"

"I won't," Steve said flatly. "I wasn't backing out on you at your office this morning. I wasn't backing out tonight. It's just that I won't go back past the day I came into this basin. I wasn't in the war. I wasn't a doctor. I packed a gun. A man with a loose gun is a tramp. He makes trouble. I want no more of that. I'm riding a trail — a narrow one maybe — but I'm sticking to it!"

"Just like Keown, eh?" Doc muttered. Steve was struck by the simile. He smiled crookedly.

"Yes," he said softly. "Very much like Keown —"

"What chance has a store man or a home-steader got against a pack of short-grass guns, Lewellyn?" McKenna said with rising anger. "You think about that!"

He stepped with emphasis on the cigar still glowing on the ground and turned back toward the Barnage house. Lewellyn passed around Barnage's little corral and took the wagon track through the weeds toward the hotel.

Chapter 12

Approaching Jed Barnage's store along the wagon track, Lewellyn saw lights were up in the living quarters behind the *Courier* office. He remembered that Sharon had said she wanted to see him. She must have known in advance, as Zoe had, of the offer the town planned to make to him if Keown proved intractable. Likely she had been concerned that he would accept, that what she had built up in Keown would be displaced, destroyed. He considered knocking on the back door of the *Courier* building, then thought better of it. He would see her in the morning.

But thinking of Sharon turned the emptiness of the night back on him, the surety with which Brokenbow was drifting into an eddy of violence, and the taste for a drink was suddenly in his mouth. He veered from the wagon track, intending to cut around Barnage's store and go up through the lot beside it instead of waiting until he reached the hotel. A barrel hoop in the weeds snapped up and stung his shin. He kept his eyes down after this, and for this reason nearly walked into John Devore before he saw the man a few yards farther on. The faint odor of whisky drifted from Devore's direction. The man was standing in the thickest of the weeds. He had a lighted cigarette between his lips and was staring off across the lots. Steve realized Devore had not seen him.

As he watched, the printer drew suddenly and heavily on his smoke. The fire at the end of the cigarette glowed up, lighting a bloodless, frozen face. In the same instant, Lewellyn saw Devore was clumsily holding a huge pistol in his free hand. Like a shuttle Steve's mind strung it all together. The lighted window back of the *Courier.* Keown with a new problem to face. Sharon with her concern and her devotion to peace. The old top-buggy back of Barnage's store. Devore. His face. The gun.

Lewellyn started forward as Devore flung his cigarette down with a muffled oath and lunged out across the lot. Steve lengthened his stride, running a dozen long steps as lightly as a cat. He caught Devore's coat by the slack under one arm and pulled him up short.

"I'll go with you, John —" he said softly. And he tried for the gun.

Devore did not turn his head. He barely glanced back. With a fierce strength he jerked free and lashed clumsily with the gun. Lewellyn rocked on his heels and jerked an arm up, but the heavy steel barrel came on through. It rang loudly against his forehead just under the slant of his hatbrim. He staggered, trying to keep his feet, trying to reach the man in front of him. He tried to shout. He failed in both of these things.

He went to his knees. He could hear Devore churning on through the rank growth toward the buggy. He forced himself up and ran unsteadily after the printer.

The buggy rocked violently as Devore approached. Ord Keown spilled out of it — without his coat. Sharon bent under the top, with her foot on one rusty step bracket. And she screamed:

"John, no!"

Devore jerked awkwardly to a halt. He ignored Sharon. He faced Ord Keown, two yards away.

"You thieving bastard!" he said thinly. And he flung the big gun in his hand upward. A gesture of complete and senseless fury.

Keown moved instinctively. Sharon cried out a second time. The sound was cut short by the flat jolt of Keown's belt gun against the night air. Devore lowered his outstretched arm slowly. He said something in a choked voice which seemed to be his wife's name. His loose frame unhinged and he fell. He was dead when Lewellyn reached him. Keown turned to Sharon, above him on the buggy step.

"He jumped me too quick!" he said with tortured defensiveness. "I didn't have time, Sharon —"

Lewellyn scooped up Devore's gun and reached Keown in a stride. He pulled the man roughly around and reached past Sharon into the buggy for Keown's coat. He thrust the coat into Ord's hands, along with Devore's gun.

"Lock this in your safe," he said swiftly. "Give me your gun. Get back to the office and get yourself another. Get on your rounds. Get out of here. Quick!"

"I had to do it, Lewellyn," Keown said mechanically. "You know that. I had to stop him. . . ."

Sharon stepped on down to the ground. She was at Keown's shoulder.

"Do what Steve says, Ord," she said in a strange, flat voice. "Get away from here, now!"

Keown swung full to look into her strained, white face. A searching look. It lasted a long moment. At its end he reached into the buggy for his hat, dropped it onto his head, and walked rapidly away, pulling on his coat as he moved.

"You should have said something to him — something more than that," Lewellyn said quietly to Sharon. She glanced at him but made no reply. Steve took her arm, steering her clear of Devore's sprawled body. The weeds mercifully hid it before they had gone a dozen yards. Sharon's step faltered. She halted. Steve stopped. He was standing there in the darkness with Sharon leaning heavily against him when a man came trotting cautiously down the far side of Barnage's store, saw them, and veered in their direction. Steve saw with relief that the man was Christoffersen. Alex came up with curiosity wide on his face.

"Devore is out there by that buggy, Alex. His gun is with him. Get hold of Doc, will you? And keep it quiet. This has been quite a shock to Mrs. Devore. She — she couldn't quite reach him in time —"

The lie was convincing. Steve was careful that it should be. Alex backed a little away.

"Sure, Lewellyn," he said softly. "Sure thing. I was — ah — I was outside. I thought I heard a shot. I'm sorry, Ma'am. Terribly sorry."

Alex moved off through the weeds. Steve glanced at the windows in the quarters back of the *Courier* and led Sharon toward the light burning there. The door was not latched. It opened into Sharon's kitchen. Tidy except for a bread plate with a little butter on it and an open bottle of indifferent whisky, both on the table under a window. Steve found a glass, spilled a generous amount of whisky into it, and pushed it into Sharon's hands. That it was Devore's whisky made no difference now. He thought she needed it.

The stove was still warm. A pot of coffee sat on a back lid. Steve opened the grate door and slid in a couple of pieces of wood from the box behind the stove. He shook the pot to be sure it held enough coffee. When he turned around, Sharon was still holding the glass of whisky, untouched.

"I don't know who to send around, Sharon," he said. "Somebody. Ruth Barnage would be best, maybe. She'd come closest to understanding. Or Jennie Westfall."

Sharon shook her head. She glanced at the

chair across the table from her.

"Sit down, Steve," she said quietly. "Why pretend? You're expecting me to make something of grief. I'm not going to. How can I when there isn't any? Pity, I guess. Even anger at John's stupidity. But not grief. I can't be that dishonest. Not with myself. Not with you."

Lewellyn reached around and found himself a glass. He idly poured himself a drink from the bottle on the table. He raised it and looked at Sharon across its rim.

"Something like this had to come, Sharon. You knew it," he said.

Sharon shook her head.

"Not something like this. So foolish. So — so — damned foolish!"

"You're stubborn," Lewellyn said. "There's gut in even a coward, somewhere. Even in John. Even he could hackle up when what he had was being taken away from him. If it wasn't you, it was his pride. You'd know which."

"What he had — !" Sharon's bitterness roughened her voice. "From me? Nothing. Nothing, Steve, since the first weeks. Hate, maybe. Scorn. Nothing else. And for that he tried to kill a man!"

"What did you expect him to do — make room for Keown in his bed?" Lewellyn said acidly. "Like Keown's trying to make room for Hal Fenton in Brokenbow?"

"Of course not. I'm not the first woman who hated her husband. There are laws and customs.

All of them on John's side. None of them measuring the things which living with him robbed me of. Laws and customs giving him the right of it. Saving his pride. He could have left me, even ordered me out. He could have divorced me. He should have — a year ago, two years ago. Long before I ever talked to Ord Keown. But he didn't. His judgment was better than the law's. His hands were stronger. Violence was his due. Is death what he wanted, then?"

Lewellyn shook his head.

"I don't think so, Sharon. I don't know what he wanted. But I think I know what he didn't want. He didn't want Keown to have you. This was the sure way. With luck he'd get Keown. If not —"

"If not — that's it, Steve. That's the reasonlessness of it. John poured his life on the ground, wasted it. What is between Ord and me now?"

Steve stood up. He deftly slid his gun from its holster and dropped it on the table in front of Sharon.

"This —" he said bluntly. "The same thing that was between us in La Mesa."

She touched the gun with the same compelling aversion with which she might touch death itself.

"You see deeply, Steve," she said. "This is going to be hard for Ord. I tried to back him up. I can't now. You're right. I think he's going to need you."

Steve shook his head again firmly. "I'm not a woman."

"It's gone beyond that, Steve," Sharon said, looking up. "I'm not just thinking of Ord. I'm thinking of the town. It's yours too. Ord can't hold the lid on alone. He's going to need help."

"Who's going to say where the lid fits?" Lewellyn asked sardonically. "Who's going to be judge, jury, and executioner? That's your God talking, Sharon." He lifted his gun from the table. "This is for trouble in my own yard. That's all. I can't change gods twice in a lifetime —" He swung toward the door. Sharon pushed her chair back swiftly and crossed to him.

"Steve, if I could believe you'd changed at all —" she broke off with an effort. Her voice dropped wearily. "Thanks for what you did out back. Thanks for making Christoffersen think — oh, it had to be that way! There's enough against Ord now. He couldn't have that. Not now. John killed himself. It's true, really. But will it stick?"

"I told Alex to see that it did," Lewellyn said. "It will." He pulled open the door and stepped into the night.

Christoffersen was idling on the street. He crossed rapidly to Lewellyn.

"Charlie Bissel's got a pair of stiff ones all poured for us at the Grant, Steve," he suggested. Lewellyn nodded. They crossed to the saloon together and bellied to the head of the bar, apart from the rest of the trade. As they lifted their glasses Christoffersen brushed against Steve and dropped something into his pocket. Steve's fingers went in after it, felt the pin and the serrations on the edge of Keown's badge.

"I found it in the buggy," Christoffersen said quietly. "Everything else is all right. McKenna got a couple of boys to carry Devore down to his place. He didn't see nothing wrong. You know Mrs. Devore a long time?"

Steve swallowed the whisky. It was not his regular brand. It burned. He choked a little.

"A long time," he agreed. His tone seemed to tell Christoffersen all he wanted to know.

"I told you I didn't know many of the folks here," the Swede said thoughtfully. "Tonight was the first time I'd ever been to Barnage's house. But I'd seen his girl on the street plenty. That was some dress she was wearing tonight!"

"She wore it for me," Steve said.

"I know," Christoffersen admitted uneasily. "I bought you this drink to tell you something. I saw you go out the back way at Jed's. And then McKenna. I wanted to see you both. I followed you. And then that dress. Miss Barnage was still in the arbor after you left. I said hello. And we got to talking. She told me about the dress — and you, Steve. That's where I was when I heard the shot behind Jed's store."

"Well?" Lewellyn said.

"I'd like to go back, Steve. I asked her to wait."

"Tonight?"

"Tonight. She wanted to know what I aimed to build on my section when I had all my fencing up. I'd admire to tell her."

Steve understood, then. It wasn't the dress. It

234

was Zoe. He laughed. Reaching in his pocket, he rang a dollar down on the bar.

"You do that, Alex," he said. "You do that and I'll buy the drink."

Christoffersen grinned widely and drained his glass. Steve touched his arm.

"When you get back to Jed's, ask Jennie Westfall if she'd mind coming down to the *Courier* office. Sharon ought to have somebody with her tonight," he said.

Chapter 13

A peculiar lethargy kept Lewellyn in his bed long after the explosive rising of the sun. The rising stir of movement on the street before the hotel and the sounds which came up from it seemed distant, unreal, meaningless. Lewellyn felt apart. He lay wide-eyed on the bed while the room slowly became warm with the touch of the sun. For a while he imagined it was the thought of John Devore, dead in a box in Sock McKenna's front room, which worked on his mind, fastening the end of every thought to its beginning so that each was a tight circle of small radius, going nowhere, without conclusion. But honesty denied this. Devore had been born with his spirit on its knees within his body. An inner smallness had discounted his physical bulk. There had been meanness and petty savageries, magnified by the spongy fears with which he lived. He had lust for nothing beyond the hungers of his belly and his body. His death had been inevitable. Perhaps Ruth Barnage had touched upon it. Life was not a strong current within him. Even in expiring fury it had thundered only faintly. Lewellyn felt no regret for John Devore, no sympathy.

Keown was in his thoughts also. A small and

polished and diamond-hard man who walked thin ice of his own contriving because of a woman. A skilled, lethal, emotionless man who was destroying himself to support the fallacies of a woman's thinking. A man who would not understand that a woman might not find the same pleasure in the hardness of his soul as she did in his hard body. Keown would believe that the identity of a dead man had shattered the night-grown tower he had built with Sharon Devore. He would not understand that it was the inflexibility of long-schooled habit within himself that had shattered it. He would think he had changed. But he hadn't. No man could, beyond certain limits. This Lewellyn understood.

And Sharon was in Lewellyn's mind. A remembered vision of a nakedness as clean as the green grass on the banks of a pool on Willow Creek. A girl backed with the tail of her skirt unconsciously raised to the welcome heat of a glowing stove in a sweat-salted bunk shack. A woman.

Lewellyn tried to see wantonness in her, but he couldn't. He could see only stubbornness. A kind of magnificence, with which she set new points for the compass which guided the conflict of men's affairs and tried to swing the needle to them by the strength of her convictions alone. Courage. Concessions, unwilling and physically painful, perhaps, to the same strong hungers and the same seeking of kind for kind which had made Lewellyn too controlled in his three years in Brokenbow, too finely whetted and absorbed in himself — which had made him drink almost too deeply of the warm and heady wine Zoe Barnage had poured out to him in her father's arbor.

Out of all of Steve's thinking in this stuffy room with plaster cracks overhead and the smell of lint under the bed, only that which touched upon Zoe was complete. Alex Christoffersen had not seen Zoe's dress in the arbor as Steve had seen it. To Alex, the dress had been beautiful. And his thinking was not so large it couldn't be contained within the boundaries of the life for which Zoe Barnage was bidding so eagerly.

Lewellyn dressed slowly. For all his thinking, he knew why this morning was different from others, why he was reluctant to meet it. The answer lay within himself. He had refused McKenna and the others their open enough request for his gun, his boots on their walk instead of Keown's or in addition to them. And with a conviction that his judgment was sound. A conviction that he could not revert to the sureness of his days on the *llanos*. He had been in Kansas too long. A determination that he would not revert. Those years were behind him with their bright, hard moments of sometimes empty victory. No town was worth the look Sharon had given Ord Keown as he stood above her husband's body with a smoking gun. No town was worth the destruction that look had worked in Keown's soul.

So the reluctance was this: it was a little unfamiliar and a little hard to see friends grow wary of a common foe and hitch their belts forward and step their own walks lightly. It was hard to see, without letting the sharpness and the clarity of judgment and perception which was an anticipation of violence and the spinning die of luck run through him. He was empty, and the emptiness was because he was without the needling lift of excitement which comes with one man's challenge laid down to another across the width of a dusty street.

Kei Lin was not in the restaurant when Lewellyn came in for a heavy mid-morning breakfast. Lin's wife, a round and perspiring Mexican woman, was behind the counter. She served the meal without comment. Lewellyn ate slowly. Returning to the street, he tried the door of the *Courier* office. It was locked. He passed down the side of the building and tried the door of the living quarters in the rear. This was also locked and the kitchen blinds were drawn. Sharon was not there. Going back to the walk, he stepped into Barnage's store. Jed was in his chair at the desk behind a counter in the rear. He swung around, gestured at the end of the counter, and pushed some empty cartons off another chair.

"Sit down, Steve," he invited. Lewellyn shook his head. "Stand up, then," Jed said, unconcerned. "Reconsidered?"

"No," Steve said.

Jed frowned a little. "Thought maybe you'd seen Ord this morning. Figured maybe you'd thought better of your answer, after that."

"Keown?"

"He's busted his seams, Steve. Can't quite figure it. You was out back of the store last night. Was Ord there?"

"Christoffersen was there, Jed. Did you ask him?"

"I did," Barnage agreed. "Caught him as he was riding out before breakfast this morning. He said no."

"Won't that do, then?"

"Guess it'll have to. Steve, we've got to have you. I got to make it personal if asking won't do."

"I'm sorry, Jed," Lewellyn said. "I've held you my best friend here. I've had few, anyplace. I owe you something for that. And Ruth and Zoe. Maybe McKenna and some of the others. But my gun is mine. I'll not hire it."

Jed's lips compressed.

"Then you didn't come in here to buy some shells?"

"No. I asked Alex to see if Jennie Westfall wouldn't spend the night with Mrs. Devore. I was by the *Courier*. It's locked. I thought I'd find Jennie here and she could tell me where Sharon had gone."

"Out to Tie Creek, Steve," Jed answered. "Jennie's been wanting to look to the corn out there. Thought she might be able to do something with it. And it seemed like a good thing to get Devore's wife out of town today. They took Jennie's kids and my wagon. They'll be back for supper."

Lewellyn nodded thanks. At the door he turned directly up to the livery, saddled his horse, and rode out the Tie Creek wagon road. The tracks of Jed's wagon were fresh in the dust before him. He lifted his pace. But Jennie had apparently made an early start. He did not see the wagon until he reached a little park a mile below the head of the valley, where Westfall's section lay. And it was headed back to town, rolling fast and with Sharon driving. There was a peculiar urgency in the way she swayed on the seat, working on the team with the tag end of the reins.

Steve touched spurs and went forward at a full lope. When the wagon was almost to him, he shouted. He had a feeling that Sharon would have driven on past him without seeing him if he had not done so. She jerked in the seat, leaned back with her weight against the reins, and sawed Jed's sweat-streaked team to a halt. Sharon had been more than preoccupied with her driving. She was angry. A white, compelling fury which drove all beauty from her face, so that it was a bitter mask of tense muscle and white lines. Puzzled, Steve turned to Jennie Westfall for explanation. He found it.

The farm woman's face, on the side turned to him, was blue and swollen, the huge bruise pulling her features out of all proportion. She sat the seat with a peculiar woodenness as though still stunned by a blow. One of the kids in back was sobbing fearfully. A wide-eyed little girl had her skinny arms around this smaller child in comfort and her eyes were bright with open hostility as she looked up at Steve.

"What happened?" Steve asked softly.

Sharon shuddered. "Steve — Steve! If this could be Willow Creek again, just for an hour —" She stopped herself. Some of the wildness went out her eyes. "Steve, I'm sorry. That wasn't fair. Come on, ride back with us to town. I'll tell you."

Lewellyn put his hands together hard on the pommel of his saddle. He saw that Jennie Westfall's dress was torn across the back and a long scratch ran down one arm.

"Tell me here," he said.

"No, Steve. This isn't for you —" Lewellyn bent from the saddle. He had guessed half of the story. It was enough to roughen his voice sharply.

"Don't be a fool!"

Sharon put the lines down. "Hal Fenton lied to you all last night," she said wearily. "His new herd isn't eighty miles away. It wasn't then. It's on Tie Creek, Steve. And so are most of his men. We saw them when we came into the bottoms. Jennie's corn was gone. There isn't a strand of fence up. But Jennie hadn't been up there since the fire. She wanted a look at the ashes. She wanted to find something — anything. The big, bucktoothed rider they call Curly stopped us as we were getting out of the wagon."

Sharon stopped, breathing heavily. "Steve, I never saw anything like it in my life. It was Jennie's land and she had already been hurt. I don't think she could even feel. She wouldn't stop."

"He hit me!" Jennie Westfall said softly, without sharpening her vacant gaze.

"He knocked her down like she was a steer!" Sharon exploded. "And the rest of them making side bets. I had to lift her into the wagon while they settled them. I'll kill that man myself if he ever sets foot in Brokenbow!"

Lewellyn backed his horse. "Turn around, Sharon!" he said.

She looked up quickly. "No! Not alone, Steve. There's men in town who can handle this —"

"Turn around — !" The words cracked like the frayed end of a bullwhip.

Sharon picked up the reins and wheeled the wagon. The crying youngster in back fell silent. Lewellyn rode ahead. They came this way into Westfall's valley. Steve saw the new Willow Creek herd numbered a couple of thousand head. He saw also, with mechanical attention to detail, that half of the riders scattered around the perimeter of the herd would have to stay in position to prevent it from breaking. They couldn't come in. He rode straight on to the chuck-wagon beside the foundations and ash of Westfall's burned house.

Four men got up from under the trees, walking curiously and with truculence into the sunlight. Foremost among them was the big-framed man Alex Christoffersen had cold-cocked the day before and dragged from Steve's own barn. Next behind him was a smaller man whose face was vaguely familiar. The other two hung in the fringes of the shade — forty-and-found riders waiting for the wind to blow before they guessed its direction. Steve rode up to within a pair of yards of the one called Curly.

"Did you hit this woman?" he asked the man softly. He jerked his head in the direction of Jennie Westfall. The man looked at the wagon and then coolly lifted his eyes to Lewellyn.

"Brother," he said solidly, "that ain't a woman! That's a genuine, razor-backed she sodbuster. She come off that wagon and put an ear-bite on me before I'd blinked both my eyes!"

"Take off your gun," Lewellyn said. The man grinned insolently.

"I don't think so!"

Lewellyn shrugged and palmed his gun with a wicked swiftness in the middle of the movement. "Make up your mind, Curly!"

The Texan's grin faded. He moved his hands slowly, unthreading the double-lap of his embroidered belt. He let the weapon and the leather drop, stepped away from them. Steve unsnapped his own belt, swung down, and walked backward toward the wagon until he could hand both up to Sharon. He gave her his gun.

"Take Curly first if any of them move," he said.

He started forward. Curly waited until he was a yard away, then drove in. He hit Steve twice, jolting, hard blows to his body, before Steve was close enough. Steve kept his hands high, forcing the Texan's drive down against the saddle-stiffened muscles of his belly, and he hit only the Texan's face. It lasted less than five minutes, a time in which neither man made a sound. Curly was still conscious when Steve backed away from him, but he could not get above his knees without toppling over. His nose was broken and hammered into complete shapelessness. Both eyes were closed, wide gashes over his brows letting skin and lids sag down over them in a bloody welter. One ear was ragged, torn loose from his head at the lobe.

He hung on his knees, his body rocking back and forth like the head of a bear with a bullet under its spine. When Steve was belting on his gun again, he spoke thickly.

"I'll kill you for this, Lewellyn!"

A grin wholly without humor parted Lewellyn's lips.

"Maybe," he agreed. "You can try, Curly."

The smaller man, who had stood behind the Texan, lifted his battered companion to his feet.

"If Curly misses, I won't, Lewellyn!" he said. "You put a slug through my kid brother's leg when his back was turned yesterday. Ask about Sid Miller before you give me a brash answer!"

"I've heard about the Miller boys," Lewellyn said softly. "Hal Fenton is hiring high-priced men this trip."

He lifted into his saddle then. Sharon, white-faced and silent, followed his movements with a strange thoughtfulness. Lewellyn nodded at her. She lifted the reins, wheeled the wagon, and started toward the foot of the valley. Lewellyn rode without concern behind it. On the streets of Brokenbow, in a saloon or on Whisky Row, or somewhere along the road one day, he'd meet Curly or Miller or another one of this crew who had a fast gun and a yearning for grassland fame. They'd trade their shots with him then, and they'd try to kill him. But they'd let him ride away, his back to them now. It was part of a vain code, an old code. And maybe a warped one.

When they were out of the wider valley and again into the little park in Tie Creek's lower cut, Sharon pulled up the wagon. Lewellyn saw that although Jennie Westfall's face was beginning to give her pain, the woodenness was gone out of it. The simplicity of the gratitude in her eyes embarrassed him. Sharon saved him from the halting words forming on the farm woman's battered lips.

"Steve," she said slowly, "I never enjoyed anything quite so much in my life. I don't think anything ever made me feel quite so good inside!"

Steve looked at his knuckles. They were stained.

"Why?" he said. "It was bloody."

"It should have been!" Sharon said with feeling. "And I know what made it good. That man had no more chance with you than Jennie had with him."

"Off-the-cuff justice," Lewellyn said shortly. "It usually works that way."

Sharon nodded slowly.

"Yes," she agreed. "Yes, I suppose it does. Steve, talk wouldn't have evened that score, would it? Lawyers wouldn't have evened it — argument couldn't have. Curly will remember the feel of your hands longer than he would a fine."

"He won't have much of a face the rest of his life," Steve admitted.

Sharon was leaning far forward on the seat of the wagon. Pleading came into her eyes.

"Willow Creek ranch has got to have something like that to remember, doesn't it, Steve? Something to remind it that Brokenbow wanted peace, but that it would fight for its rights — for its existence. If Hal Fenton had been given something like that to remember in Long Draw, maybe dad would still be on Willow Creek instead of in a grave in Abilene. Maybe Fenton wouldn't be on Tie Creek now. Isn't that what you tried to tell me once?"

"Once. But it doesn't make much difference whether Pete Lynch is buried in Abilene or La Mesa. It doesn't make much difference who's in Brokenbow. If it wasn't Fenton it'd be another drover off of the *llanos*."

247

"But if Fenton was beaten — bloodily, Steve, like you beat Curly — the others would walk lightly. They'd keep their hands off of the town and the fences on the ridge. There'd be no more seeing how far they could go, how much Brokenbow would give —"

"Look," Steve said bluntly, "you're Sharon Lynch. Remember? Sharon Devore. You ran away from the *llanos* because there was blood on them. You're the *Courier*, in Brokenbow. You're the girl who's going to pull the teeth of the devil himself with a tin star, a couple of calfskin books, and a smile. You're forgetting —"

Sharon shook her head again, fiercely. "I'm not forgetting, Steve!" she said sharply. "I'm just seeing, just understanding. For the first time. There's wrong and right. There isn't any compromise. It's lie down or stand up. I want to stand. I want to see Brokenbow stand!"

Lewellyn thought of what McKenna had said, about a fence down the middle of a man's vest. Now Sharon was saying it. It had been Sock McKenna's belief. He wasn't sure about Sharon. Steve had said a man could not change. He doubted if a woman could more easily.

"Steve, I've been a fool," Sharon continued intensely. "I wouldn't listen to you — when I wanted to, terribly. And I've done something to Ord Keown — something to Brokenbow. You've got to help me. You've got to!"

Lewellyn shook his head.

"Go to Ord," Sharon went on, the words coming more swiftly, more urgently. "He'll listen to you, I think. Take it in your own hands, Steve. Help Jed Barnage and Doctor McKenna. They're right. Let them stand up. Stand up with them. Match Hal Fenton. Steve. Match him every move. Use your gun. I cleaned it for you a long time ago. The day you fell in Willow Creek. Use it, now!"

Lewellyn jerked so sharply on his reins that his horse reared a little.

"This isn't the *llanos*, Sharon," he said harshly. "This is Kansas. I told the same to Doc McKenna. I'm telling you. This isn't the short grass. This is a town. Half a pie and an appetite is better than a whole pie and a bullet through the belly. Fenton will make a deal if he isn't crowded too far. I'll tell Ord that. I'll even string along with him on it if he keeps his hands open. But I don't sell my gun — to you or to Brokenbow!" Sharon straightened. Tears swam above the lower rim of her eyes. The distillation of desperation.

"You're afraid of Hal Fenton, Steve. And I thought John was a coward!" Her voice was soft, acid, unsteady with repression. It stung. It hurt. Lewellyn fended off the hurt, clinging grimly to his own conviction about this woman. A conviction as steadfast as the heat she engendered in him and the emptiness.

"You're angry," he said quietly. "Maybe not even at me. At Curly. And you're talking out of anger. You're not thinking. Tomorrow you'll be the same as you were last night. And you'll remember what I did to Curly up there. It'll be something else you'll turn over in your mind, along with Charlie Bissel's money and Banta and Les Macambridge and Randee Fenton whenever you think of Steve Lewellyn. I'm not adding anything else!"

Sharon stared at him for a long moment.

"It's not me who's the fool, after all, Steve," she said very softly. "It's you. What do you know about what turns over in my mind — in here —" she crossed the high, full firmness of one breast with her hand "— when I think about Steve Lewellyn . . . whenever I've thought about him since the day he left La Mesa? What do you know about the loneliness and bitterness that made me marry John or the desperation that made me listen to Ord Keown? What do you know about me at all?"

"What I remember," Steve said. "I'm splitting off, here. You can get the wagon on in. Look now — Jennie fell, taking a youngster down to the creek for a drink. Let it go at that when you get into town."

Westfall's wife had sat silently on the seat beside Sharon, her head lowered and her swollen eyes closed. She straightened sharply now and her voice came up in a protest of surprising strength.

"So Ruth Barnage will put a poultice on my jaw and say, 'Poor, clumsy Jennie!'? Not on your life! I got my hooks into a damned ornery critter back there and scratched the daylights out of him before he knocked me down. You can run from your own bite if you want to, Steve Lewellyn, but I won't help you. So long as one man ain't afraid, the whole town's got a chance. Jed Barnage and the Doc are going to like what I've got to tell them!"

Sharon smiled suddenly, undefinably, at Steve and flicked the reins in her hands. The wagon rolled forward.

Chapter 14

Alex Christoffersen was in the Grant when Steve came in, slapping the dust of his ride up Tie Creek from his jacket. Christoffersen grinned a greeting.

"I paid up another day on your room at Kinner's, Steve," he said. "Thought I might like to share it tonight."

Steve put an edge into his protest, a part of his quarrel with Sharon Devore yet left in him.

"I'm wound up in town. I'm going out home soon's I eat!"

Alex shook his head. "You stick to an idea when you get it, don't you, Steve? Listen, I was out to my place today. I rode back by way of yours this afternoon. Hal Fenton's boys weren't eighty miles away last night. They were at the head of the valley. There isn't a strand of fence left up from the head of Tie Creek to the main ridge. My shack is down, knocked flat. There isn't a fit stick or pan in yours. We're down to blue chips, Steve, whether you want it or not. It's fight or run!"

Lewellyn put a hard, jolting drink down inside of him and turned wordlessly toward the door. Christoffersen followed him onto the walk. Jennie Westfall had returned Jed Barnage's

252

spring wagon. It was at the rail in front of Jed's store. Zoe was just helping her father into it. She saw Steve and Alex and called to them both. Steve glanced at Christoffersen and angled across the street with Alex still at his elbow. As he moved he saw Ord Keown come out of the Spur and halt on the edge of the walk. Jed, now in the wagon, took off his hat and ran his hand through his thin hair as they came up. He barely glanced at Christoffersen. His eyes nailed down Lewellyn.

"Alex has told you how the upper valley is, Steve. And you know what happened to Jennie, today. Now what?"

"I'll know better than to leave my place again," Lewellyn answered steadily. "Jennie'll know enough to stick to the counter in your store."

Jed flushed darkly.

"By God, Steve, I've had about enough of that! About enough of you —"

Zoe cut in hurriedly. "Dad thought sure he'd be able to sell you some cartridges now, Steve."

Lewellyn swung on her. "All right, Zoe," he said carefully. "You promise me that a week from tonight I'll look the same to you — to every other woman in Brokenbow — as I do now, and I'll fill my cartridge belt!"

Puzzled, not understanding, Zoe glanced uneasily at Christoffersen. He gave her a quick, reassuring nod, but she still didn't see what Steve had meant.

"How can I answer that till the week is gone, Steve?" she asked cautiously. Steve grinned flatly.

"You can't," he said. "That's why I'm riding up the valley tonight when I've eaten!"

Zoe looked down at Christoffersen again, then lifted the lines and clucked to her team. Steve watched the wagon move up the street. Ord Keown came along the walk, striding with exaggerated steadiness. He stopped at Steve's elbow. His half-lidded eyes also followed Barnage's wagon for a moment.

"I heard that, Lewellyn," he said. "You're crazy! You never made a trade of your fast gun. How come it sets you so heavy now?"

Lewellyn made no answer. "I've made a little powder-smoke talk along my back-trail here and there," Keown went on. "I've used it. I get paid more for the echoes of that talk than for the work I do. Always have. But I'm not trying to bust off my trigger-finger, like you. What's it mean? You think you're a better man than I am?"

Steve pulled his eyes from the street. This was what Jed Barnage had been talking about in his chair in the store this morning. Keown's seams were showing. Ord was drunk. As coolly, methodically, completely drunk as the man's habitual thoroughness could contrive.

"With a gun, Ord?" Steve asked. "No. Nobody could touch you behind sights. I'm sure about that if not the rest. It's just that I don't want to stand over a dead man somewhere in this

254

town and watch the woman I want walk away from me. That's all."

Keown blanched like he had been hit. Christoffersen sucked at his breath with an audible gasp. For a moment Keown stood teetering on his heels, his body slack and his eyes dead mirrors. Then a strange, bloodless calm seemed to settle over him, not erasing the white strain on his face, but letting the tenseness out of his hands and arms and shoulders.

"You won't, Lewellyn," he said quietly. "A man has got to pull a gun to shoot anybody with it!"

Keown strode on up the walk. He passed the Spur and turned into the smaller Wagon Wheel. Christoffersen stirred beside Lewellyn.

"Your fur must be parted the wrong way today, Steve," he said softly. "You hit Ord where his big hurt lives. You should have forgotten Devore. I think Ord might have swung with us if the Texans tried to plow too big a furrow. Now, I don't know!"

"Go ask him, then," Steve suggested angrily. "But get off of my heels. I've put my mark in the dust. I'm standing on it!"

Christoffersen did not appear to take offense. He shrugged and moved off. Lewellyn headed straight for Kei Lin's restaurant, thinking that at the counter there he could avoid the condemnation he felt building against him along the street. But the Chinese was party to it also. The supper he served was flat and tasteless and the round humor of his face was flattened grimly. Anger at the town and the people began to grow in Lewellyn. Anger at Sharon Devore.

He had hid nothing from the beginning. He had left the *llanos*. He had left what Sharon had despised in him there. At least he had tried with all the singleness of purpose of which he was capable. He had made nothing of his gun in Brokenbow. He had filed land and anchored himself to it. These people had accepted him as a homesteader. They had made themselves friends. They had let him forget in a measure the empty bitterness of his departure from La Mesa. In a quiet time they had done this.

Now, when they faced trouble, they wanted this all back. They wanted him to wear his belt as he had when he had ridden into Willow Creek. They wanted him taut and edgy, walking the middle of a dusty street with eyes which trusted no one, not even them. They wanted to see him and marvel at him and set him apart because they feared him, because death rode his hip. Sharon had shaped him. A better and more lasting job than any woman could do on Ord Keown because Ord's shallowness had been built for defeating women. Now Sharon wanted to destroy what she had made and begin again. It was too late.

He paid his tally to Kei Lin without comment and went again onto the street. Doc McKenna was plowing up the walk in front of Cragar's store, two doors away. Lewellyn stepped down into the dust, angling circuitously toward the Grant in an obvious effort to avoid head-on meeting with the flame-headed little Scotsman. McKenna did not raise his eyes. He passed on up the walk without apparent notice. This also rankled. Steve had changed direction deliberately to force McKenna to hail him, and the man had not done so.

There was wisdom in Doc. Lewellyn had wanted to hear his voice. He had wanted to talk. McKenna was inflammatory, but his flames were steady and steadying. Steve hit the doors of the Grant with a black bitterness growing within him which took into account no living man but Steve Lewellyn. If this was the old pattern, disavowed and forgotten, recurring as though it had never been mastered, Steve did not fight it.

He was standing before his third drink with his heel hooked over the rail of the Grant's bar, staring at Charlie Bissel without seeing him, when Hal Fenton brought his Willow Creek crew back into Brokenbow. The drovers made a quiet influx. They came in two detachments, from both ends of the street, riding abreast its width from walk to walk. Steve felt the beat of many horses through the planking of the Grant's floor and watched them from the doorway. There was something admirable in the completely unhurried convergence of the two parties, in their practical confidence. Fenton had brought a carefully chosen two dozen veterans of the longhorn trails to accomplish his work in

Brokenbow. They were sober, armed, and primed to a man. Big Curly rode beside Sam Dreen. Lewellyn tasted brief pleasure in the dark, swollen ruin of Curly's face.

The majority of the riders turned nonchalantly in at the long rack before the doors on Whisky Row, four of them swinging down a pair of yards from the place where Lewellyn stood. Charlie Bissel touched Steve on the arm. Turning, Steve saw only the night-lamp was left lit in the big room.

"I'm going to try to get closed up, Steve," Charlie said urgently. "Go out the back way if you want, but pull the door tight after you!"

Lewellyn stepped out onto the front walk for an answer. Behind him Charlie Bissel chuckled with a sound which was almost friendly and said:

"Careful, farmer!"

Steve heard the door go shut. One of the Willow Creek riders heard it too. "One down, boys," the man laughed. Others laughed with him. Steve walked unhurriedly along under the awning fronting the Grant. Passing one window he saw Charlie, carrying his under-counter gun, setting the lock on the back door from the inside. Up ahead another man afoot crossed the walk and stepped out into the middle of the street to face Fenton's second force coming in from the other direction with Fenton at its head. Steve halted abreast the narrow opening between Charlie Bissel's building and the one next to it. A breath of air, coasting down from the ridge, passed through this little alley, striking his face. Hal Fenton pulled his bunch to a halt and called out to the man who had walked into the center of the street:

"That you, Keown?"

"Yes."

"What you want?"

"I'll take an answer to that first, Hal," Keown answered.

"All right, Marshal," Fenton agreed easily. "We've finished a drive and we're thirsty. Twenty-two of us. Twenty-two. Object?"

"This town is like any other, Hal," Keown said evenly. "Business feeds it. Your boys can ride in here with their guns off and drink us dry if their cash holds out. But there's no use looking for trouble. That's something we don't stock in Brokenbow!"

"No?" Fenton asked mockingly.

"No," Keown repeated. "We don't have any. We don't want any. I can prove it. I've got to have a couple of your boys, Hal. The one that knocked three of Jennie Westfall's teeth loose today. And one out of the bunch that pulled down eight miles of fence and broke into two houses in the upper valley."

Lewellyn's tightened nerves flinched for Keown. He knew the strain. This was sand. This was guts. If courage could make justice stand on its own legs, then justice was out on the street now. But justice didn't have legs. Only a man had two to stand upon. And this man was alone.

If Sharon was watching, if she could hear, maybe she could understand now what trading for right and trading for principle could come to sometimes. Even courageous trading.

"We could have made this come out all right, Ord," Fenton said.

"It will now," Keown answered. "Give me Sid Miller and Curly Bower, Hal. Then buy the rest their first drink — on me."

Fenton turned in his saddle. Lewellyn saw that Miller rode a rank behind his boss. He didn't see much else. Keown held his eyes. The marshal of Brokenbow was no longer drunk. He was beyond hurt. He had escaped Sharon as Lewellyn himself could never escape her. Every fiber of his being, every pulse of his mind had shortened focus until there was only himself, the street, and the Texans. This was his work. He lived it. He was even beyond being a strong and forceful man. He was a machine. Fenton swung back to face Keown. It could have been a signal, prearranged. A gun put its sound down on top of everything else on the street. A gun fired from the darkened knot before the Grant.

Keown wheeled without evidence of having been touched, dropped to one knee for steadiness, and fired three times with incredible rapidity. Three men went down on the walk before the Grant, making the threshing sounds of dropped animals. The others in the group broke, racing for shelter. One came loping down the planking toward the place where Steve stood

260

in the shadows. As the man reached him, Steve chopped the barrel of his gun down, tumbling the drover onto his face. He leaped the man's body, took the hitching rail with one hand to lift him, and landed at a full run in the street.

The Texans behind Fenton broke their ranks, clearing the street except for their milling horses, and their guns opened up. Dust geysered around Keown, bent over the knee he had used to steady his gun. Lewellyn judged the marshal had been shot cleanly through in the first volley. But out in the dust was no place for a man with Keown's nerve to die.

Keown saw him coming and pulled himself to his feet, unable to completely straighten the kink from his belly. Lewellyn picked him up where he waited without slackening his own crossing run. He hooked a shoulder under Ord's arms and half dragged him across to the other walk. Lead from two directions took out a window in the *Courier* office, directly in front of them. Lewellyn kept low, reaching up to cut one whistling swipe of his gun barrel against the lock on the door. The hasp sprung and fell free. He tripped the latch, sliding inside with Keown beside him. A close one came off the face-plate on the latch of the door and burred angrily between them, its sound hitting Steve's nerves like that of a circle-saw on green lumber. He hit the gaping door with his elbow, slamming it shut, and dumped Keown onto a chair. Ord stirred, pulling at his coat.

"Through the ribs," he said tightly. "A lot of

blood coming out. Can you get a compress on?"

Lewellyn ducked back into the quarters behind the office, too hurried to wonder where Sharon was, and found a drawer of linen. He stripped the first piece which came to hand, ripping it into two wads and a long binder. Keown put his arms up. Steve found the wound, front and back, by its tenderness and the wetness of Keown's shirt. He crammed the wadding on, wrapped the binder as tightly as he could, twice around the man's body. Ord put his hands down to the chair back and hoisted himself, standing steadily. His eyes circled the office.

"Funny place for me to be!" he murmured. "Look, Lewellyn, you'll see her. She's always been yours and I should have known it. You'll see Sharon. Tell her I tried. God damn it, I tried!" Keown took a step toward the front door, punching fresh shells into the cylinder of his gun with practiced economy of attention and effort. Lewellyn caught his shoulder.

"Not alone, Ord!" he snapped. "You won't get across the street!"

Keown rocked his gun up. Steve couldn't see his face in the darkness.

"Get out the back door, you fool! You can stay the way she wants you. Get out of here. You've done your part and you haven't fouled your barrel yet. I bit off too big a mouthful a minute ago. That's all. It'll go easier now. It'll have to."

Steve heard the hammer set back on the weapon in Keown's hand. He pulled his own

262

gun free and reached for the door. There was a quiet in him, now, letting his breath come and go in steady rhythm. There was no more argument with himself, no more balancing of principles, no more of the *llanos* or of Kansas. Not even of right and wrong. Brokenbow had one hope. It lay with two men only, the marshal of the town and a man from the short grass who could not change his stripe when the last card went down. One man and his principles weighed lightly against the future of a town — so also did one woman. The door came open in his hand.

"Split when we hit the walk!" he said to Keown, and he lunged through the frame.

Chapter 15

There were two stone buildings in Brokenbow, the post office and Jed Barnage's store. Keown started down toward the post office at a quick walk, holding himself flat along the fronts as he moved, becoming in a dozen paces a swift, dark shadow in the heavy gloom under the awnings over the walk. Lewellyn wheeled in the other direction toward Barnage's store. Keown was obviously making for the shelter of the post office, planning to use it from which to drive out the six or seven drovers left at the lower end of the street below the Grant. A heavy rifle had begun to smack steadily from one of the windows at Barnage's. The *Courier* was empty. Steve thought Sharon was with Jennie Westfall at the hardware store. But he had to be sure.

As he hit the corner of the *Courier* building he saw Sam Dreen dodge from the shelter of a horse at the rail across the street and scuttle toward the space between the buildings housing the Wagon Wheel and the Spur. Sam had forgotten to hang his bad arm in a dark sling and the white patch of flour sacking across his chest winked like a light. Lewellyn snapped a shot down at him. Dreen went flat, sliding across the walk to ram his head against the wall of the Wagon Wheel. But he

264

didn't stay. He made a thin, strained cry as he came up to his knees. Sam was a bad customer, even one-handed. Lewellyn wanted him down for keeps. But somebody broke the glass out of a front window in the Spur, thrust his gun out, and drove a splinter from the building against his back into Steve's neck. At the same moment the door of the Spur opened. Sid Miller and a man whose face Lewellyn couldn't see reached out. They caught Dreen up as he reeled along the walk and yanked him inside. The man in the window of the Spur laid another shot in too close to Steve.

Lewellyn bent, snapped at the window, and ducked back along the side of the *Courier* building at a full run. Coming into the open at the rear, he swung toward the back of Barnage's store. Behind the stone building he saw the team and wagon Zoe Barnage had driven down the street earlier, pulled into the shadows. He let his stride out, forgetting the street for a moment. Passing behind Kei Lin's restaurant he saw a light within puff out at the beat of his steps.

Ruth Barnage had a shotgun leveled at the door when he came in the back of the store. Jennie Westfall's wide body was blocking the door to the front of the building. She was reaching new, tagged guns down from a dusty rack and stacking boxed shells by each. She turned, saw him, and grinned. Ruth Barnage put the shotgun down.

"Which way you running?" she asked, and

Steve couldn't tell whether the strain in her voice was sarcasm or a vain reach for humor. Zoe tumbled down the ladder from a balcony where hand-tools were stored. She was carrying a heavy posthole bar.

"Ma —" she said. Ruth took the bar from her, drove its point into the floor and wedged its bit against the back door. Zoe touched the floor. She looked at Steve.

"You knew they'd come like this?" she asked. Steve pushed past her without answer and nodded toward the front of the store. "Who's out there?"

"Jed —" Jennie Westfall said. "Where's Sharon?" Impatience made him sharp.

"Home —" Jennie Westfall said. "That's where she was going —"

"She's not there," Steve said. He moved on into the front of the store. A bullet from the street had punctured a barrel of coal oil. Its smell was strong in the air. Jed was sprawled out flat, shooting over the raised window-box to one side of his front door. He had three men caught behind an old wagon box in the open between the Wagon Wheel and the livery, and he was holding them there.

"How is it, Jed?" Lewellyn asked above him. Barnage didn't lift his head from the groove of his rifle sights.

"They're filtering in. Ganging up in the Spur and maybe the Wagon Wheel. Somebody came up the back way on the other side. I tried for 'em

266

and missed. Good thing. It was one of our boys. He picked off at least one behind that wagon when he went by. Then hell busted loose back of the Spur. I don't know what — now!"

"Mrs. Devore's outside somewhere. Seen her on the street?"

Jed shook his head. "Lewellyn —" he said, "— there's a horse in my barn — if you want it —"

"The hell with you, Jed!" Steve said. He returned to the back room. A hammering commenced on the back door as he came in. Zoe backed against the wall, picking up one of Jennie's rifles from the big wrapping table. Ruth Barnage lifted her shotgun again. Steve raised the posthole bar which braced the door and pulled it open. Sharon Devore stumbled through the opening, her face ashen. She swept the faces confronting her until her eyes touched Steve. She took a step forward and fell against his chest.

"Steve!" she said faintly. "Somebody said you had gone before they rode in. Steve, it's terrible!"

"You little fool!" Lewellyn said raggedly. He pushed her over to a little stove in the corner of the storeroom. "Here, get a fire going in this. Ruth'll tell you where there's a pot and fixings. These folks can do with some coffee if this runs very long."

Sharon gripped a lifter and dully raised the single lid on the stove. Steve crossed to the door. Zoe Barnage put down the rifle in her hands and seized his arm.

"Steve, find Alex. Find him and get back here," she cried. "Get back here and make dad get out of that window in front. It isn't worth this. It isn't worth it! This damned little town! This mean little clutter of boards and dust isn't worth one man's life — and you'll all be killed! Find Alex and come back, Steve —"

Sharon turned at the stove. She spoke softly, but her voice rang.

"It's my town, and yours, Zoe. Your mother's and Jed's. Steve's, too — and Christoffersen's. It's worth anything —" She paused, looking again at Lewellyn. "But Steve, do come back —"

Lewellyn pulled the door open, swung it closed behind him again. And as it swung, the brief, narrowing beam of light from it fell on the body of a man sprawled not twenty feet away. Steve bent beside it, lifting the man's head. It was Cragar. Half of the man's blood was on the ground under him. He wore no belt and no gun. A crushed sack of eggs was beside him. It was plain the mercantile owner had locked up and just started home when the drovers rode in. A stray bullet from the explosion on the street had caught him here.

Lewellyn raised, waited until Jed Barnage started his sporadic fire with the big rifle in the front of the hardware again, and broke into a fast, light-stepping run. He came out to the street beside Barnage's window and angled across the dust toward the wagon box behind which Jed had holed three men. He almost

268

reached the far walk before the guns in the Spur and the Wagon Wheel started on him. But by that time he was changing his angle so rapidly they couldn't follow. He plunged across the walk, heartened by the slam of a lighter weapon in Jed's other window. Jennie Westfall, he thought. Cutting sharply around the corner of the Spur, he dived into the high weeds along the railroad embankment there.

A sharp voice stabbed at him: "Alex?"

"Lewellyn, McKenna," he answered. "Where is Alex?"

Christoffersen's voice came in softly from the left. "Right with you. Hold it, Steve. I'm coming over."

Singly, they crawled up to him. McKenna, Kei Lin, and Christoffersen. The Swede slammed a big, flat hand against the curve of his back.

"You bastard!" he said with feeling. "We figured you'd gone down out there in front, with Ord, when he walked up to take his medicine!"

"He took it and walked away too," Lewellyn murmured.

Christoffersen whistled softly. "So it's him in the post office, then! He hasn't wasted a shot, either! That end of the street's clean, best I could see from where I was. I think they've all moved into the Spur. We've pretty well shot the back wall out of the Wagon Wheel from here. Doc thought it was Cragar in the post office. His house is up that way —"

"Cragar's dead," Steve told them.

McKenna stirred. "We'll all be if we don't get a lid onto this!"

Kei Lin grunted and lifted his counter gun. "Is having four shooting-shells left."

Lewellyn saw they were all waiting on him, accepting his change and his presence without comment. Asking no questions. Waiting for his judgment, deferring to his experience.

"All right," he said rapidly. "Look, Alex, Zoe's at her father's store, sick from looking for you. Jed's alone with the women. Go back the way I came and help Jed cover the street from his windows. Doc, you and Lin work up as close as you can to the back of the Spur. When the thing starts out front, shoot the back door clean into the place. And save some spares if they make a break in your direction."

McKenna growled sourly. "I didn't crawl out into these damned foxtails for a back seat!"

"You've got it!" Lewellyn snapped. "But it'll be smoky enough. I'll swing on up where I can get hold of Ord before he caves in. It won't be as bad as it looks now. Maybe one or two of Fenton's boys are good enough, and know it, to stand up to anybody. The rest of them are working for pay, not glory. They'll break. Give us luck and the right timing and we'll empty the Spur."

"You make a dog out of me, Steve," Christoffersen protested quietly. "Sending me down to the women!"

"I told you Jed was alone with them. I said Zoe

was there. Wait till you see her face and you'll know why I sent you."

Doc McKenna leaned forward. "Devore's wife is there too, isn't she, Steve?" he asked quietly, but with unmistakable meaning.

Lewellyn stood up, ignoring the question.

"Lewellyn, you're a damned fool!" Doc murmured with conviction. Christoffersen also came to his feet, his hand out. "Good luck. Steve —"
Lewellyn touched the hand and started down the tracks. Fifty feet away, back of the Grant, another man rose out of the weeds. Another man with a shotgun.

"Steve!" Charlie Bissel breathed. "I was afraid you were missing. I been watching the other side for you."

"Ord still in the post office?"

"No. We're clean at this end. He came out. He's along the other walk somewhere, between buildings. Where's the rest?"

"Back of the Spur. Get down with them, Charlie. They know what's coming."

Bissel nodded and started up the same track Lewellyn had come down. Steve turned up the south side of the Grant, searching the opposite wall of the street carefully. It would make a difference if he couldn't find Keown. It would make a difference if Ord was down. The shooting of a gun in this kind of a thing was never so much a question of accuracy as of nerve. The finality of death was close to every man when guns were talking. Those who had no apparent fear of it, or control over their fear, had steadier hands. And Keown had nerves of iron. Two of them cut the odds on the street in half.

Steve spotted Ord finally. He was standing in the mouth of an alleyway between the *Courier* building and Kinner's hotel. He tried to catch the man's attention, but failed. Giving up, he broke suddenly and sprinted across the street without drawing fire. Keown was looking at a man between his feet. A pudgy little man breathing with the slow laboriousness of a punctured lung. Ord glanced up to the balcony over the hotel veranda.

"Kinner," he said. "Must have nailed him up there. He just spilled down. Almost on top of me. He's finished."

"You all right, Ord?" Lewellyn asked. The marshal grimaced wryly and nodded. "I'm going for a walk," Steve went on. "Coming?" Ord smiled thinly with anticipation.

"I've been waiting for you," he said.

They started along the walk. Keown did not limp. He didn't drag. But it was an obvious effort, controlled and deliberate. They moved abreast along the planking, keeping the street between them and the front of the Spur, until they were nearly opposite Lowell's saloon. Guns opened up from the windows of the Spur, but a heavy fusillade from the front of Barnage's store shortly silenced them. Steve grinned, Alex would have had time to reach Barnage's now.

He'd keep the street open from here on. Christoffersen knew how to fight.

Keown stopped for a moment, gripping an awning post for support, before they stepped into the street. He glanced apologetically at Lewellyn. After a moment he straightened.

"Seventy-five feet —" he said softly. And he stepped out.

Lewellyn found himself thinking of the distance also. Three feet to the step. The gap narrowed. They came up on the other walk. The door of the Spur stood before them. In the last stride Ord Keown forced the sag from his body and shoved suddenly ahead, so that he was into the doorway a fraction of a moment ahead of Steve.

The remnants of Hal Fenton's short grass crew were in the room. Every man was turned toward the door. Six, maybe seven, maybe eight. They fired simultaneously. Ord Keown shuddered. His body was flung roughly against the frame of the door. He half turned, his nails biting the frame for support as he knees sagged.

"They're expecting us, Steve!" he breathed.

Lewellyn did not see him fall. His eyes photographed four men. Hal Fenton was behind an overturned table, his face level with that of Sam Dreen, who sat on the floor behind the same onyx-topped shelter. Curly Bower stood a little forward toward the center of the room. Sid Miller was behind the bar. These four Steve took into account. No others. Bower's gun jerked again, so that the shot he had flung with the rest at Keown and that which struck Steve made but one elongated explosion.

It was fair shooting; it was a fair try at fulfilling the promise Curly had made the day before on Tie Creek. Steve held himself up against the shock of the bullet, leaning into it as a man will lean into a strong wind. So long as that feeling of having pressure against which to lean lasted, Lewellyn knew he could keep on his feet. After that . . .

He didn't watch Bower. He didn't know where he hit the man. It didn't matter. Curly went down and that was enough. Sid Miller had his try too. But the caution which had put Miller behind the bar made him a little slow. His shot went wide and he didn't have time for a second. He put his gun down on the bar in front of him. He lowered his head as though to look at it in astonishment. He slid from sight as his knees buckled.

A man a little to one side of the overturned table behind which the wounded Dreen and Hal Fenton were crouching suddenly wilted as he leveled his gun. Steve saw with detached clarity little holes leaping into being in the partition which separated the bar section of the Spur from the back rooms and he judged Bissel and McKenna and Kei Lin had turned loose. He flung a shot against Fenton's table top. The stone turned it with an upfling of powdery dust.

A cross-shot from a nameless rider somewhere

else in the room caught under Lewellyn's shoulder blade, gouging a deep bite, in and out. It pulled him around in a full turn, so that he faced the door. In that instant another man drove into the Spur. Steve knew he must have been only yards behind Keown and himself when they hit the door. This was a crazy man. He wasn't cool like Keown, like Steve Lewellyn. He was swearing savagely and with pleasure. He hit the door at a full run and held on across the room toward Hal Fenton without breaking stride. Steve forced himself back around, planting his legs wide, and he shot Sam Dreen through the head as Dreen came up from behind the table for a hurried shot at the big Swede charging toward him.

Christoffersen shied from the table then, catching two of Fenton's men in a corner of the room. He shot one of them clumsily and hastily and drove the full weight of his body against the other, pinning him to the wall. The man broke like an egg. The door in the rear partition flung open. Kei Lin's counter gun dimmed the lamps with the jolt of its concussion. Hal Fenton stood up behind his table, bent, and slowly folded over its up-turned edge like a frayed and empty suit of clothes.

McKenna and Charlie Bissel were at Lin's shoulder, mirroring his grin. The grins died. Steve knew the three men were looking at him. He knew Alex Christoffersen was motionless in his corner, staring also. He turned slowly, and

275

started for the door. There was a stir. McKenna's voice spoke, sharp with command:

"Let him go!"

Lewellyn touched the framing of the front door and found his way through it. He turned on the walk, with the night wind on his face, and found the rail back of the hitch rack. The front door of Barnage's store swung open and figures ran up the street. There were women among them. Beyond the women was the livery. His horse was there. But it was too far. Too damned far. He gripped the rail tightly. Zoe Barnage hurtled past him. He heard the impact of her body against Christoffersen near the door. He heard her quick breathing and her young voice flinging the big Swede's name joyously against the night, over and over:

"Alex!"

There were two bullet holes in his body. They hurt. There was a bitterness which hurt also. A culmination of the restrictions and the hurt and even the hatred he had for this town on the Kansas prairie. An accumulation out of the three years he had forced himself to stay within the boundaries of its narrow horizon of fences and thinking. The building he had done for a woman, in shards in an hour. The faith he had kept through three grim years of honest effort burned away as swiftly as powder, because in the end he had known no other answer for Brokenbow.

He did not see Sharon. He did not hear her.

But suddenly she was there beside him, before him, her body in his hands instead of the initial-scarred pole of the railing. Her voice was not like Zoe's. It was softer. Deeper. And it did not say his name. It did not say anything. It was making only formless, meaningless sounds which had meaning, nevertheless. Her lips against his face and the salt there. Blood on her arm from the stain on his shirt.

"I told you to come back, Steve," Sharon murmured. "But I couldn't wait. I came to you — I had to come. Now we'll go back together —"

"Back?" he said thickly.

"Brokenbow will have its peace now, Steve. You made it — and Ord. We'll go back to the *llanos*. I was the coward, Steve. I was the fool. I want to go back. I want to begin again — where we left off that night on Willow Creek. Steve, take me back to the short grass. That's where the roots are. Mine and yours. That's where this had its beginning and where our beginning was. I want to go back to it — the grass and our own brand and the heat and the dust and the room to be right and sure — always —"

Doc McKenna appeared beside Sharon. He touched her arm.

"Let me help you, Ma'am," he said gently. "He's a mite heavy for you to be holding up —"

"You don't understand, Doctor," Sharon said softly. "Steve is holding me up. I'm not afraid any more —" she looked at the smear on her arm, "— even of blood. He's lifted me off my knees."

The hurt was gone out of Lewellyn. He pulled Sharon's head against the vee of his shirt with one arm.

"Why don't you mind your own business, McKenna?" he asked. The Doc chuckled softly.

"I'm trying, boy. But damned if I can patch a man up if he won't lie down!"

HD DMS